HERE IS THE BEEHIVE

HERE IS THE BEEHIVE

SARAH CROSSAN

LITTLE, BROWN AND COMPANY
New York   Boston   London

Little, Brown and Company
Hachette Book Group
1290 Avenue of the Americas, New York, NY 10104
littlebrown.com

First North American edition November 2020
First published in Great Britain by Bloomsbury Circus, August 2020

Little, Brown and Company is a division of Hachette Book Group, Inc. The Little, Brown name and logo are trademarks of Hachette Book Group, Inc.

The publisher is not responsible for websites (or their content) that are not owned by the publisher.

The Hachette Speakers Bureau provides a wide range of authors for speaking events. To find out more, go to hachettespeakersbureau.com or call (866) 376-6591.

ISBN 978-0-316-42858-3
LCCN 2020934369

1 2020

LSC-C

Printed in the United States of America

For Mum

PART ONE

The only way
        out
        now
is to stay busy,
so I have borrowed
Anna Karenina
from my mother and will not
allow myself to cry
until I have read it.

Twice.

∾

It was ten o'clock in the morning.
My tea had cooled in the mug.
I wanted another biscuit.
I wanted to message you.
I was sorry for the argument.

                              Very.

Helen buzzed through.
          'I have a Mrs Taylor on the line.
          She says we wrote up her husband's will
          and he's passed. She seems fine.'

I scrolled through emails:
clients, questions,
an L. K. Bennett sale.
          'Put her through,' I said.
          I reclined in my chair,
          ready to be soft, supportive.

'Mrs Taylor, Ana Kelly speaking.
Firstly, let me say how terribly sorry I am for your loss.'

'That's very kind,' she said.
On my second screen
I searched Taylor in the database.
Twenty-two clients.

'May I ask your husband's first name?'

'Yes, of course, sorry. Umm … '
She was unsure,
like a name might be out of reach,
already stashed away on some high shelf.

And then.

'Connor Mooney.
I'm his wife, Rebecca Taylor.
We have different names.'

The wife.
His wife.
Your wife.
The wife.

             She had discovered us.
This was her way of getting in touch,
               of punishing me,

because you were not dead,
        we had spoken only days before.

        I was planning to message you after lunch.
        To apologise. Make things good again.

        Rebecca was calling because she knew
        and I needed a story to explain it.

Quick. Quick.
Think. Think.

'He passed away on Tuesday,' she said.
'My brother-in-law suggested I phone.'

You're lying, you fucking cunt bitch,
     I didn't say.
You're fucking lying, you bitch cunt,
     I didn't say.

I said, 'Goodness, I'm so sorry.
That's awful news.
I have his details here in front of me.
We drew up the will a few years ago.'
     My hands hadn't moved.
     I was scanning the list of Taylors.
     Keith, Leonard, Meaghan-Leah.
In my throat was an ache, hot and heavy.
My right hand twitched even as I clutched
the desk to steady it.
           I didn't believe her.

'The funeral is a fortnight this Friday.'

'Thank you for calling.
You must have a great deal on your plate.
And please don't worry about the legal end of things
unless there's a problem paying for the funeral.'

'That won't be an issue,' she said defensively.

'Well then, I'll call you afterwards.
You could
          come into the office, perhaps.'

'I'll wait to hear from you.'
She spoke like we were arranging a dental appointment,
with a calm I could not understand,
yet similar to every bereaved spouse I'd known,
setting aside grief for the brief moments of legal dealings.

I took shallow breaths.
'Do you know how to register the death?'

'My brother-in-law is dealing with that.'
She coughed hard into the phone.
I wondered whether she was wearing black.

'As executors to his will
we can assist with administration, so do ask.'
Rebecca coughed again.
I considered asking if she was sure.

                              Wholly.
                              No doubt.

Maybe it was someone else.

'Is there any more I can do for you, Ms Taylor?'

She paused.
Was she going to confess to the joke?
None of it was true. Was it?
You were going to call minutes later,
frantic and found-out.
'No. Thank you though,' she said.

'One last question. How did he die?' I asked.

Rebecca told me, briefly, all about it.
And I told her, quietly, how upsetting it sounded
and how impossible it was to be without him.
'Yes,' she said.

I ended the call
 and bought a pair of shoes in the online sale.
        Purple suede. Pointy toes.
        Impractical.
        Unaffordable.

Then I did something
                    very bad
and got back to work.

Tell me.
        What would you have done?

                    ❧

It is contrarily cold.
I am wearing a cashmere cardigan
        over a long grey dress,
        a vest beneath.
It is a Marks and Spencer look:
high-street ordinary,
plain to the point of being a blur.

I caught myself in the mirror
on the way out today,
hated the woman
you would see if
you sat up and took a look around.
        Wouldn't that be just like you?
To spy
and later
perform a post-mortem of the service –
fidgeting children,
the state of your mother's face,
thoughts on how I behaved,
the analysis exhaustive:
I liked your hair up.
You should always wear lipstick.
Could you see from the back?

I haven't eaten in fifteen days.
I haven't seen you in twenty.

I don't know when I'll next have an appetite.
I won't ever see you again.

I am as thin as I was at the beginning,
when every duplicity
                    pitched my guts.
You would say I look fine.
But I do not.
It has been noticed.
The partners seem worried,
like I might not outlive my clients' muddles.
Nora bought me a bottle of Floradix.
Tanya asked if I was pregnant.

The sun is straining through the clouds
and it should defeat them
because it is July after all.

I am holding on tight to a bunch of white carnations.

You never mentioned a fondness for flowers
but soon you shall be carpeted in
brightly petalled
dying colour
                    as a mark of love.

How do *you* smell now?
Are your nails long?

St Mary's car park is crowded.
I cannot see your coffin.

But I see Rebecca,
your boys,
all staring into nowhere.

We plan for death,
make sensible decisions while gorging on life.
But no one intends to die.

When you wandered into my office
three years ago,
you never thought
I would have to confront your family's grief,
or my own.

You thought you had forever to make mistakes
and make amends.

Your sons are dressed in suits,
standing in a row like a little black staircase.
I turn my back on them.
I am not responsible for their sadness
though that's what I've wanted.

Wouldn't it have been better than this?
Wouldn't it have been better my way?

❧

'Will Mrs Mooney be writing up a will with us?' I asked.
You were in trainers for that first meeting,
an overcoat better donated to charity than worn.
'My wife didn't take my name and
I'm pretty sure she's made meticulous plans
for her own death.
My death too, probably.'
        Your laughter filled up all the space,
        right into the dusty nooks.

We went through it:
                personal data,
                property,
                pension.
I knew your entire life fifty minutes after we'd met,
while you knew nothing of me
apart from where I'd been to university:
        I spotted you studying my walls –
        certificates of accomplishment,
        praise for a girl I scarcely remembered.
        She was ambitious,
        liked Manic Street Preachers,
        sucked off her jurisprudence professor for a first.
        Silly girl.

At the end, you loitered,
       traced circles
       on the desk
       with your thumb
and, grinning somewhat, said,
'I guess I'll be back for the divorce.'

I lidded my pen,
               left a space for you to speak.
It was January after all,
       a busy month for break-ups and
       scrounging around for grounds
       after the hellish togetherness of Christmas.

'We're here for anything you need,' I said.
I wasn't being suggestive.
I was a professional
       with certificates on the wall to prove it.
         A Bristol graduate.
'My colleague Tanya Kushner
is an experienced family lawyer.
I can ask the receptionist to make an appointment.'

'Oh, Rebecca would never let me go.
Who'd put petrol in her car?'
You rose.

'Once the will is ready you can
pop back in and sign it,' I said.
'We'll provide witnesses.'

'How lavish! I look forward to it.'
You put on the tatty coat.
A bottle of Ribena poked out of a pocket.
'Are you Irish? With the surname Kelly you must be.
Unless you married particularly well.'

'I was going to ask you the same.'

'Both parents from Meath. Yours?'

'Mum is from Cork.
Dad is from Cavan.
No one can pinpoint which town.
We all agree he was running from something.'

'Aren't we all?' You winked then shuffled,
ashamed to have done it,
reaching for the door handle.
'Have a good afternoon.'

I ate lunch alone at the Subway a few doors down.
A slice of cucumber fell on to my lap and
I noticed a ladder in my tights,
was glad I'd been sitting for most of our meeting,
was worried you'd spot me in Subway.

So you see,
even that first day you were
slinking around
                    inside,
stirring things up.

But.
Actually.
I didn't think much more about you until we met by chance
two weeks later.

You were with Rebecca.
And, oh,
            she was everything.

ॐ

How can we know which days
will be the turning points?

So long as we live,
we gamble.

Red.
Black.

Put it all on Number 11.

∾

A man is by my side. 'Ana?'

He is handsome. Bearded. 'Mark?'

'Jesus. Is it a good idea for you to be here?'

Mourners in cars search for spaces,
ways to reach the crematorium
without having to cross the road and
traipse the length of the cemetery.

A woman strides towards us and relinquishes a child
like it's nothing more than a bag of groceries.
'He needs changing.
I'm getting a lift with Sheena,' she tells Mark.

I hold out my hand to her but she is gone already.
We watch her go.
'I'm sorry,' he says. 'It must be …
I don't have a clue how it must be.
Shit, I suppose.
I've thought about you a lot.
         How you're doing.
But you shouldn't have come.
Did Rebecca spot you?'

'Does it matter?' I ask.

He pats the child, who gurgles something
combining complaint with contentment.
'I better deal with this one.'

Beneath my feet,
wet leaves cling to the tarmac.
The air smells of evaporating rain.
        In the block of council flats
            next to the presbytery,
a girl is waving from a top floor window
as though we have all come to see her.
        In her arms, a naked baby.

'Meet me,' I say.

The church bell tolls twelve.
Cars edge away.

        You will be smoked,
            nothing but ash in an hour.
I will still be in this cashmere. In these tights.
        Later I will load a washing machine,
            measure detergent into a plastic lid.

'I can't,' Mark says. 'Meet you, I mean. I can't.'

'You're the only person who knew about us.
I have no one else to talk to.'

He clicks his tongue,
looks suddenly young, accused and guilty.
'I have to think about it.
Rebecca's in bits,' he says.
Before I can ask why that's relevant
he scurries off,
velvety vomit
                    dribbling down the back of
his trench coat.

Rebecca
            in
                    bits.

People in pieces all over the place.

ↄ

I was ordering
            another bottle of
            Rioja from the bar,
Tanya shouting for peanuts,
and there you were,
fingertips on my wrist. 'Hello.'

I didn't recognise you in the suit,
shaven and smelling of influence,
and was bored of swatting men away.
I retrieved my hand from the bar,

wanted to get back to plotting with Tanya,
making plans to start up on our own:
           Kelly and Kushner Solicitors.

'I'm Connor. I was in your office a few weeks ago.'
I liked your eyebrows,
your teeth, the canines jutting forward just slightly.

'A trust dispute!' I announced.

'Last will and testament,' you corrected.
From the fug of noise
                       Rebecca emerged,
pale-lipped in a Patrick Swayze T-shirt.
She had the arms of a tennis player,
the mouth of a politician.
'Rebecca, this is Ana Kelly. My solicitor.'

I was tipsy.
Yes.
I was tipsy and nothing was rooted to the spot.
I wanted you to hold me up,
help me back to the table,
sit with me
and divulge everything you had ever been.
I stopped myself leaning in
and resting my head against your chest.

I wanted Rebecca to be more obvious.

'My boozy friend's waiting for wine,' I pointed.

'We'll get our drinks and join you,' Rebecca said flatly.
'No other bloody seats.'

Tanya rolled her eyes, opened the Uber app.
'They look like the fucking Muswell Hill set.
I can't sit and listen to the merits
of Ed Sheeran and oat milk all night.'

'Ten minutes,' I promised.
I hoped it would be longer.

You wandered over,
                    waving the peanuts
              I'd left on the bar.
Rebecca sat on my left,
              you on my right,
and she told us about the house you'd redesigned.
        You were the architect,
        she worked on interiors.
        It had all been 'taxing beyond'
              but 'God, so worth it.'
Rebecca had a way of simpering
when she spoke that gulped all the
elegance from her face;
I gazed into my glass, embarrassed by it.

You didn't look at her much,
        didn't touch those lean arms,
        instead described a deprived Catholic childhood
        and subsequent rise to success
        in a forged Irish accent
        that made me order more wine.
        You'd grown up on the Haringey Ladder,
        went to St Aloysius,
                which, even back then, was a road to better things.
        I'd dated a boy from the same school,
                one I'd met in confirmation classes
                who couldn't understand his own hard-ons,
        apologised for them and repeated over and over,
                It'll deflate in a tick
                It'll deflate in a tick.
        And you knew St Michael's Grammar,
        where I trekked each day from Wood Green
        to get my holier-than-thou education.
        'So you were a smarty-pants then?' you said.

I nodded.
        Tanya yawned.
        Rebecca adjusted her wristwatch.

'What were your sixth-form haunts?' you asked.

'Donnelly's in Turnpike Lane mainly.
They sold only booze and crackers.'

'They did!'

'And there was the one and only
O'Rafferty's with Shebeen out back.
I loved that place.'

'I worked there!' You half stood to announce this.

'What a dive!' I screeched,
knowing your pride wasn't about where you were from
but who you were now,
                          how different it all looked.
And I was your witness.   Rebecca your prize.
'It's all boarded up now, you know.
To let. When I drive past
I get sentimental for some reason.'

'Do you live close to it?' you asked.

'Not far. Ally Pally. Still trying to escape North London.
Well, I did leave for uni but came back.
Remind me where you guys live.'
Rebecca was tapping her teeth
against the rim of her empty wine glass.
'Hampstead Garden Suburb,' she said sharply.

When Tanya got bored of being ignored
and eyeballed me,
we made our excuses.

'Christ, she's dull,' Tanya said, walking me to the bus stop.

'He's alright though.'

'A bit of alright, you mean.
And he likes you.
Hampstead Garden Suburb though?
Basically they're from East Finchley. Tossers.'

Undeterred by the time or my heels,
I walked part of the way home,
          the whole length of Fortis Green
          until the balls of my feet throbbed,
and, taking my shoes off in the hallway, I thought,
    Connor Mooney, I like you too.

                 ∾

'Sorry I'm late,' I say.
      'Anything important come up?'

Tanya scampers out of her office looking horrified.
'What's with the burka?'

'It's from Cos.'

'I didn't know they sold burkas.'

I pull off the tights and dump them in Helen's bin.
She is wearing earphones and hasn't noticed my arrival.
'I had a thing,' I say.

'Fair enough. But Graham was going mental.
Apparently you missed an important client meeting.
I said you had a migraine. He wasn't buying it.'

'I forgot we'd rearranged that.'

Tanya has a look that is new:
                    examining,
                    almost benign.
'Your roots need doing.
You look like crap.'

Helen unplugs herself, sees me.
'You had about a million calls.
Everyone seems to be dying.
And you missed a client.'

Those who loved you, or liked you,
or with whom you were mildly acquainted,
are gathered together while you burn.
          I have had to flee
          at the very moment you are vanishing,
          embrace invisibility again.

Even my attendance at the funeral
you would have judged a transgression –
making myself real,
       getting
       too close
       to those you did everything to protect.

'You're not my boss, Helen, so drop the attitude, right?'

I slam closed my office door.
A minute later, Graham smashes it open.
In his right hand, a half-eaten boiled egg.
'Oh, afternoon, Ana.
Delighted you've pootled into work.'

'Sorry. I'll call them. I had something.'

'No doubt.'
He leans over my desk so I can see down his shirt,
          dark hair on white skin all the way to his waist.
'Your phone was off.'

'Yeah. As I said, sorry.'
The egg stinks.
Graham takes a bite, crumbled yolk sticking to his beard.
'Look, do you fancy grabbing a coffee?'

'No. No, I fucking well don't, Graham.'

He pushes the last of the egg into his mouth, turns,
and giving me the finger for good measure,
leaves.

∾

Witnessing the will took minutes.
'I was hoping to discuss another matter.'

I closed the door. 'Go on.'

I didn't have to feign interest as I did with other clients.
I wanted all you had.

Tell me.

And you did. About your grandfather's house in Mullingar,
how an uncle had commandeered it after his death
and getting your share looked hopeless,
unless I could help. Could I?

'Well, I know a contentious cases solicitor in Dublin.
I could give you his number.
I can't take the case myself.'

A double-decker rattled by,
passengers staring in like we were on exhibit.

I've never understood the sort of people who sit upstairs.
Even as a teenager I took cover down by the driver.

Up there was a wild place
for people not needing protection
or who were spoiling for something.

The office door opened and Tanya's head appeared.
'I thought you were free, sorry.
I can't make lunch. Friday fury.'
She half recognised you and smiled. 'Hi, there.'

And we were alone again,
though I forgot what we'd been discussing,
peered at my notes.
A family house. County Meath. Dublin lawyer.
'Did your grandfather have a will?'

'If you're hungry, I'm about to grab a sandwich,' you said.

It was not a date.
It was a sandwich.

❧

At four in the morning I finally disavow sleep –
sit on the sofa in the dark,
measuring the birdsong.

> Light attacks the sky
> behind the blind.

I am not alert in the afternoons,
head on my office desk,
calls on hold.
And at night here you are,
pacing,
        chasing me,
the muddy-booted
freeholder of my sanity.

You couldn't leave because Rebecca.
You couldn't leave because Rebecca's pain.
You couldn't leave because Rebecca's pain versus my pain.
You couldn't leave because.
You couldn't leave.
You couldn't.
You. You. You.

My neighbour's alarm rings through the wall.
She is a nurse.
Slim. Polish.
Polite when she hands over misdelivered mail.
Sometimes I want to ask her if she has access to medicine.

A van idles.

The nurse's alarm reminds her to
get up get up get up.
Light movement.

You couldn't leave because my pain didn't matter.
And now look at what you've done.

To everyone.

&

Mr Young is a new client.
      The lines in his forehead seem new too.

'I have to be able to do something
about my wife going nuts
and taking him to some posh clinic in London
where it's not just leaflets
      but drugs they're giving him.
And then I have to pay for a therapist
who won't listen.
I mean,
listens to my wife spouting neo-liberal bullshit,
but not to me when I beg him to veto the pills.
Look, I don't mind buying my son Oil of sodding Olay
or even calling him Jet.
      I call him Jet.
But if they think I'll sit on my hands
like a cockless cunt
while they bury my son
like he was never even born,
they have another think coming.

I'm paying for bras.
I mean, he's twelve years old for fuck's sake.
        He believed in Santa Claus until he was nine
        and three years later I should trust him with this?
'I'm not a fascist, which is what my wife's saying.
I voted to remain.'
        He slams his hand against his knee
        and stares at the hardback books behind me.
        He is crying.
'It can't be legal.
The father has to have a word or two to say
before they meddle with his body.'

'What would you like me to do?' I ask.

'Disinherit him.
I need a will that says he gets nothing if he's a she.
Chemically and physically, I mean.'

'You think disinheriting your child will stop this?'

'Here we go.
What's happening in the world?
I don't understand anything any more.'

This is a man who loves.
I lean forward to be closer to him.

'Mr Young. I think counselling
would be the best thing for your family.
Maybe we could talk in a few months.'

He stands. Pushes the chair away.
He is sobbing now, hardly able to inhale.
'Yup. Yeah. OK. Helpful. Thank you.
Liberal hearts unite, right?
Might have known.
Could have guessed from your
                        fucking haircut.'
I touch the ends of my hair.
It is dry. Needs a conditioning treatment.
His own is long, tied up into a messy man-bun.

He charges from the office and Helen replaces him.
She is chewing on something. 'You alright?'

'Don't invoice him for that meeting.'
I rest my forehead on the desk.
'Can I have tea?'

'Why was he so upset?'

'He can't control people,' I tell her.
'Don't put too much milk into it.'

I dragged Tanya to the Bald Faced Stag
every Friday for three weeks
until you reappeared.

You didn't see me
from your stool,
            chatting easily with the barman.
I stood by you. Ordered loudly.
'It's you,' you said.

'It appears so,' I agreed.
'I thought about heading to O'Rafferty's
but I hear the bar staff aren't up to much these days.'
It was the closest to flirting I'd ever been
but it worked,
made you smirk
and offer me a drink.

'I need help with a legal problem,' you said,
a couple of hours later
when Tanya had gone home in a sulk.

I shook my head.
'Make an appointment or I'll have to invoice you.'

'I paid for the drinks.'

'Meet me in Gertie Browne's next Friday
and I'll answer anything you like.'

The bar was noisy
but there was silence suddenly
            between us.

I was trying to arrange something.

But it wasn't the kind of thing I did,
wasn't the sort of woman I was.

I wanted to explain, to say,
        I don't know what's happening to me.

You examined your glass,
'I'll make an appointment.'

'What was your question?'
I tried to be light.

It was too late.
You were leaving,
going home to Rebecca
and her chic interiors.
                To your boys.

'I have so many questions, Ana,' you said.

Apart from the computer screens,
                    my office is in darkness.
The phone rings. It's Nora.
In the background, screaming.
'Ana. You never called me back.'

'I was just finishing off at work.'

'You're still there?
I guess that's how you afford posh wellies.'
If I didn't know Nora better
I would mistake her tone for concern.

'What do you want?'
I have my teeth in a claim that
Rogers & Cowell negligently prepared a will
and now their client's kids are fuming,
heirlooms passed on to a stepmother,
known to the deceased for less than two months
and with a penchant, apparently,
for old men with clattering coughs.

'Can you get that baker you know
to make a cake for Fiona's party?
She wants a cat on it.'

'Bit of a tight turnaround, but I'll text her.'

'Seriously, go home.
You're there late *every night*.
You aren't shagging one of the partners, are you?
Do you lot get written consent before banging each other?
Just in case.'

Nora has always been funny.
When we were children, she was unkind,
         stealing my sweets with a wink,
         pinching me for the remote.
I'd laugh
at the easy way she had of getting what she wanted
by making cruelty a joke.
'I've got to finish this.'

'Go home,' she repeats. 'And get me a cat cake.
You're paying for it though. I'm skint.'

Done with Rogers & Cowell,
I draft a codicil for Mr Ward's will
to prevent his drug-addled third son
from inheriting a penny.
         These bitter legacies
                   are not virtuous work.
         They are moral judgement
         that turn on a whim.

And then I am Googling you
like I did in the early days,

as though photos used by the media after your death
can tell me more about your life than you did.
You didn't tell me enough.
        And I assumed twenty per cent of what you said was a lie
        intended to protect me.

                Mr Ward's third son will not get
                the house or the money or the vintage clocks.
                Mr Ward's third son,
                        at his father's funeral,
                will be calculating how much ketamine he'll
                        buy with the proceeds from the family home.
                He will get nothing.
                But for now
                        he gets to keep taking his drugs.

                Rogers & Cowell are insured.
                A claim against them gives me no dilemma.

Everything is a compromise.

One question: what is the payoff?

                                ❧

I tried to look busy,
prepping for court with papers and a soft-leaded pencil
instead of idly waiting.

We were meeting at Gertie Browne's
instead of in the office to discuss trusts for your boys.

'You OK for a drink?'
You snuck up somehow from behind,
though I'd chosen a chair by the window
so I'd spot you,
                    wouldn't be startled.
I was riveted by a drunk pissing
in a disused telephone box outside.
          Not busy.
          Simply waiting,
          tapping my foot to Sally MacLennane.

'I got a sparkling water,' I said,
wondering if it sounded too sensible.

You loosened your scarf, rubbed away the day from your face.
'I might get a Guinness,' you said, almost apologetically.

'You should. They usually have Tayto too.'

'God, I haven't eaten Tayto for years.
I'll get two packets.
And something stronger for you.

I can't drink alone at lunchtime.'
I hoped that meant we would be there a while.

And we were.
We were there a very long time.

·

I miss the freckles on your shoulders,
the wispy tufts of hair there
and the clean, soapy smell of you.

·

Helen shuffles into my office
eating a toasted crumpet,
butter dripping on to the carpet.
'That weirdo called again yesterday.'

'Which one?'

'The one using mystics to find his brother's will.'

'Never put him through.'

The phone rings in reception.
She bites into the crumpet
and chews with her mouth open,
ignoring the ringing.
'I made an appointment for you with Rebecca Taylor,
wife of Callum Mooney.'

'His name was Connor.'

'Yeah. She said she didn't know
why she hadn't received your calls before.'

Perhaps because I never made a call,
petrified to talk to her.
Face-to-face?
I want it.   I don't want it.

'Are you going to clean up that butter?'

'Oh, shit.' Helen scurries out.

I check my online diary.
            2 p.m.
            Next Thursday.

I have one week to prepare for Rebecca.

                              ∾

Typically, I am gift-buying at the last minute,
scrounging around a garden centre
for something suitable to give my seven-year-old niece Fiona.
They have cactuses, bushes, shrubs, trees, fruit, spades, gnomes
and wind-chimes that would nicely nettle Nora.
If I were feeling generous I'd buy a fountain,
a fat Buddha with water
trickling down his tummy,
serenity until moss begins to grow
and the useless thing stops working –
fit for a skip.
            People who own fountains
            must have little else
            to distract them.

I saunter along the rows of roses,
        blooms almost consumed by summer,
        thorns their lingering adornment,
and find myself surrounded by fencing,
latticed and bamboo –
ways to divide people.

A robin whistles from the top of
a squat olive tree.
'What?' I say aloud. 'What do you want?'

I buy birdseed and a feeder.

Nora will be cheesed off.
But then, when is she not?

∾

On a flight back from a St Patrick's weekend in Cork with Nora,
both of us stinging with hangovers,
the air steward jumped up,
        waved his hands
        in admonishment.
'Back to your seat, madam. Back to your seat.'

I only saw the woman from behind, head bowed.
'It's really bad. I have to go. I have to go,' she said.

The steward was crimson.
The seatbelt sign was on. Rules were rules.
'We're on the runway, you have to sit down.'

The woman pleaded.
'It's really bad. It's really bad.'

The steward grabbed a phone,
        waved it at her like a loaded weapon.
'Sit. Down.'

She had two humiliations to choose between,
repeated, 'It's really bad. It's really bad.'

'Let her use the toilet, you barbarian,' Nora snarled.
She was in sunglasses,
swigging on flat Coke.
Passengers shifted like they understood the woman
and understood the steward,
knew desperation
but respected rules.
        The sign was on.
        We were about to take off.
        What would happen if we did?

Watching her standing in her shame,
        begging and trembling,
        I was so grateful

this woman wasn't me,
and felt lucky that all my wrongdoing
was unknown.

Nora unclipped her belt.
'She's gonna shit herself, you dickwit.'

'And I'm going to call security,' the steward said.
'Both of you, sit down.'

'It's OK. It's OK.'
The woman turned to face every sitting passenger
and went back to her seat.

Nora sat down too.
'I think I might be dying,' she murmured.

The plane juddered, roared, and up we swept,
                    along with the starlings.

~

Mum is in the garden,
a glass of Pinot Grigio in one hand,
a can of Vapo in the other,
spraying away wasps.
'Just come inside,' I say.

'And let the little pricks win?'
She keeps her finger on the trigger.
'Can I get a top-up, pet?'

'It's eleven o'clock, Mum.
Wait until after the party.'

She holds her glass aloft.
        'Come on, be a good girl.'

The wasps advance. I pour more.
'Nothing else until later,' I tell her.

Mum sprays the air and coughs.
        'You always do what you're told.
        That's why you're my favourite,' she says.

∾

You called when you could have emailed.
'Just a quick question about trustees.
Is it a good idea to have a backup?
In case of illness or something?'

The question was inane.
The answer was yes.
I clicked off the time clock
and enquired about your boys,

45

had you remind me of their names –
Jamie (*lovely*), David (*right*), Ned (*oh yes*) –
and their ages –
five, eight, twelve.
                          I was silent on the well-being of
                                      Rebecca.

And then it was on to your lingering insomnia
since the boys were babies,
and my work-induced exhaustion.
You recommended a meditation app,
I recommended a podcast.
We agreed beer was a good cure for both
and decided a drink
soon was sensible.
'For health reasons,' you said.
'Let's expense it to Bupa,' I replied.

You laughed
and I wanted to sharpen all my words against you,
test how they sounded.

And when I laughed,
                          it rang around the room,
something rare and tempting.
No one made me laugh like that
or cared to try.

From then on,
we enjoyed one another.

Completely.

෴

Nora says, 'You're emaciated.'
Mum says, 'She looks grand, stop it.'
Nora says, 'Fiona hates the birdfeeder.'
I say, 'I gave her a tenner too,'
although it disappeared
in foam and bubbles almost as soon
as I'd handed it over.

Nora offers me a plate of sausage rolls.
'Dad's engaged to a Russian.
She's twenty-six – apparently the age
men most desire.'

Mum sniffs.
'When I was twenty-six he fancied Thelma Scott.
When I was twenty-seven it was Rachel O'Brien.
He's had more crushes than a ... '
            She hasn't the patience for a metaphor
            and begins unwrapping jam sandwiches,
            shooing children away from the
            plate of pink wafer biscuits.

I last saw my father at my graduation,
a man smaller than I'd remembered,

with uncontrolled facial hair
and big white teeth
     that looked like they belonged in a Shetland pony.
'Nice one, Ana,' he'd said,
         handing me a box.
Inside was a pearl
which, drunk,
I pressed into a stranger's hand later that evening.
It was a black pearl
no bigger than a pea
that I discarded like a copper coin.
It can't have been worth a lot.

'The cake is lovely, Ana,' Mum says.
'I specifically asked for a cat,' Nora complains.
'The baker was busy. Butterflies was all Ocado had,' I say.
The entertainer is loud, old,
dressed like a teenage skateboarder:
baggy three-quarter-length combats
and stripy odd socks.
His balloon hats keep bursting.
The hall jangles with crying.

Fiona tugs on my hand.
'Uncle Paul says I can give you back the birdcage
and you'll give me twenty pounds.'

'It's not a cage,' I explain.
'And you're not getting any more money.'

Paul waves from the corner of the hall,
where he is watching
        Aston Villa versus Liverpool
on his phone.
Jon is asleep on his knee.
Nora leans into me.
'He's great, your Paul, isn't he?'

'Dad took Mary Sands on the very same cruise
we took together a year before,' Mum says.
'First proper holiday I'd ever been on.
The gall of the man.'
I have repeatedly heard this story,
how Dad was caught
because he failed to remove the foreign currencies
from his wallet.
He couldn't pretend the Turkish lira
had been in there all year –
he'd been gifted the wallet that Christmas.

Nora waves at the entertainer,
who announces it is feeding time.

I check my phone in the kitchen.
        WhatsApp reminds me you haven't
        been seen online for weeks.
        No one has bothered to take down your picture,
        the one of you on a boat –
        your first experience sailing.

It gives me half a second of hope
that you are not dead.

Nora pokes her head through the hatch.
'Hand over that bottle of squash.
But *why* are you so thin?'

'Did Dad ever love us?' I ask.

Nora rolls her eyes.
'Please have a sausage roll.'

ॐ

I was only on my first drink
and there it was.
                    'Do you love me?'
I could have been eleven years old
for all the sense that question made.
I'd known you two months;
you still addressed me as Ms Kelly in emails;
we hadn't even kissed.

'Sexually?' you said.
There was fear and a lack of preparation on your part.
What had I expected but a defence?

We were in Gertie Browne's again,
debating the Troubles, Alastair Campbell, Brexit.
How no one seemed to give a damn
about the Irish any more.

Outside it was raining.

'I don't know.
Just. Do you love me?'
I hadn't realised I needed an
answer to this question until the words were loose.

'Well.' You looked at the door.
'I think about you when we aren't together.'
You didn't pretend not to understand.
You weren't that sort of man.
'Is that enough?'

I should have made a joke of it.
How different everything
would have been if I'd retreated.

'I need to know this thing isn't in my head,' I said.
I flipped my beer mat.

You downed your drink.
'It's late. I should go.'

You didn't touch me at all, but said gently,
'You haven't imagined it.'

∾

Inside they are singing 'Happy Birthday'.
Candles flicker and melt, are blown out,
       the warbling ends.

'Hello?' Mark says, answering the phone.
My number is unknown.

'It's Ana Kelly.
I wondered if you'd thought about meeting me.'

'Couldn't you text?
Wait a sec.'

Even when I was a child and the celebration was mine
I hated children's parties:
the screaming, chasing,
music that guaranteed parents would dance,
jammy dodgers, cartons of orange,
everyone sent home with cake wrapped in soggy napkins.

Now I avoid them because
they are too early in the day to justify booze.

'Hey. I'm here.' He pauses.

'Hi. So … ?'
I am as tentative as I was with you at first.
Afraid to say what I wanted,
tiptoeing into audacity.

'Come to Brighton for a few hours.
I'm between projects the next few days.'

I turn. Paul is at the window, watching.
I wave.
But I have been caught and we both know it.

'I'll do that,' I say.
'Why don't you text me a day and time?'

'Yeah. Bye.'

He ends the call.
I keep the phone to my ear, mouth words,
nod,
roll my eyes a little,
anything to appear business-like.

Eventually Paul steps away from the window.
I have missed my niece blowing out her candles.

I am standing in drizzle.
He disapproves.

The irony: *now* he is jealous.

～

'You're married,' you said.

I wiggled the fourth finger on my left hand,
showing off the gold wedding ring.
'I forget to wear it,' I said.

'Right,' you said. 'Yes,' you said. 'You forget,' you said.
'And you also forget to talk about him. At all. Bit weird.'

'That's because we always talk about you,' I said.

You were not happy.
The first of many betrayals.

～

Paul slams down a mug of camomile tea
                              in front of me.
Its slimy bag floats to the surface.
'You're always working.'

He has been hostile since we left the party,
and though he hasn't mentioned the call
it is there between us,
reminding him of everything I am not.

You aren't like other women,
Paul used to say, and still does sometimes,
though
        the meaning has changed.

'The partners are down my neck.
Give me a break.'

He sits in the armchair,
        not next to me on the sofa,
and I am glad,
would be gladder
if he didn't sit at all
but let me watch
David Attenborough alone.
I want to know what happens to the cubs
when a new lion enters the pride.
        Will he kill them? Chase them away?
The lioness is powerless to protect her babies.
She skulks then lets the lion impale her.
'You're so moody,' Paul says.

'I'm tired,' I tell him.

But I cannot explain how tired.
The exhaustion infects my lips, my eyelids.

Nothing twinkles or hums.
I don't know how to make that happen any more.

    Perhaps
    with you gone
I should make an effort to please Paul.
He's here
    after all
and you are not.
He made me a hot drink.

My phone pings. A message from Mark.
'I have to go in to work tomorrow actually,' I say.

Paul frowns. 'On Sunday?'

I sip the tea and turn up the TV
as a cub is mauled to death by her stepfather.
'Yes. That's what I just said.'

∾

I took your hand
as you hailed a black cab
and without looking at me
you squeezed it and said,
'We'll detour via your place.
Come with me.'
In the back
we fell into each other.
'I want you,' I said.

'I want *you*,' you said.
Mouth on mouth
hands trembling
tongues confused.
'I'm sorry,' I said.
'Me too,' you said.
We didn't stop.
I undid your shirt buttons.
You gripped my chin so hard it hurt.
'Oh, God,' I said.
'Oh. Oh, God,' you said.
Outside The Starting Gate,
opposite the train station,
on the road parallel to my own,
I jumped out
unwillingly,
wanting to find somewhere,
          a park even,
and waved cheerfully
like kissing
was nothing of consequence.

But
I didn't sleep all night,
lay hypnotised by the white wall
thinking
          what have I done what have I done

and called in sick
the next day
thinking
  what have I done what have I done.

      ∾

'Everyone loves Brighton. I don't get it,' I say.

Mark considers the pub,
like he might be able to explain
the merits of the city
by drawing attention to
the fruit machines.
'People like the sea.'

I'm craving a sticky toffee pudding. Custard.
This pub looks like the place to satisfy that need,
and I am hungry for the first time in days.
Mark nods at my empty.
'I'll get you another.'
He heads for the bar.

  I check my phone out of habit
  but you are still dead.

  You will not message me again.

'I got crisps,' Mark says.

'Does Donna know you met me?' I ask.

'Donna? Fuck, no.
She hasn't a clue about you,
        or you and Connor.
She'd call it scheming.'

> 'Mark shags around a lot,' you'd said,
> likes to have women hurt him.
> But a good bloke.
> Loyal in other ways.
> Ridiculously talented artist.'

He opens the crisps, nudges them towards me.
'I'm not sure what we're doing here,
        to be perfectly honest.'

'Was he ever going to leave her?' I ask.
My question is smudged by the ping of a cash register.

Mark leans forward. 'What?'
He has a chickenpox scar above one eyebrow,
        moles on his neck.
        In the breast pocket of his shirt is an assortment
                of pens and pencils.
        Evidence of his creativity.

'At the funeral Rebecca was acting like a real wife.'

'What are you talking about?'

He uses the rubbery end of one of his pencils
to remove a mark from the table.
'Did he love her? Did he love *me*?'

'He was lost, Ana. From day one
the whole thing was fucked.'

'And by day thirty? By day seven hundred?'
I hold out my hands,
use my fingers as counters.

'We both know it's too late to figure it out.'
He folds his coat across his lap.
                    He would like to go now;
                    I know the signs.

'I need the truth,' I tell him.

Mark sighs. He is impatient,
as if we've known one another for years
when I have met him only twice –
          once with you,
          a drunken night of karaoke,
          and then at your funeral.
'You know the truth, Ana.'

But he is wrong. I know nothing.
      Even now.
Why am I here and not at home?
      Paul will dump me.
      I will deserve it.

Mark sips his ale, touches the base of his neck.
It is an intimacy I do not need
'You want me to say Rebecca's the devil, is that it?'

'How *is* Rebecca?' I ask.

'Let's not go there,' he says,
      as you would have:
        I don't want to talk about Rebecca,
          and
        Can we leave my wife out of this?
          and
        Why does she matter so much?
          and
        Don't humiliate yourself talking about her like that.
You didn't like refereeing
      between her and me,
      Rebecca ignorant of her involvement in a battle.

I swirl my wine. My guts swim.
'I just meant … ' I begin,
but Mark shakes his head.

'I can't meet you again.
If I do and Donna gets wind …
She caught me once before.'

'Doing what? Consoling one of Connor's lovers?'

'Funny.'

A child passing the pub chases a butterfly.
His mother smiles, shouts, 'Keep out of the road!',
placidly pushing an empty pram.
        In her hand is a half-sucked lollipop.

'I know how to be without him
because of how things were, but not like this.
I can't win him back.
Or win him at all.
You know?'

Mark takes off his fedora, places it
        between us
        on the table.
'He never found your break-ups easy.
He fell apart a few times. He struggled.'

'He always seemed fine.'

'He said that about you too.'

'We only ever broke up when I'd had enough
of his indecision and ended it.
He just waited for me to crack and call him,
started trouble at home
so he had an excuse to take me back
whenever I eventually got in touch.'

The table next to us is free,
just a residue of cashews and crisps
left on crumpled packets.
            Someone has left behind a calculator.
I have an urge to clean up,
leave the space ready.

Mark leans in. 'You don't know Rebecca.'

'How do you mean?'
Finally it feels like conspiracy,
and I want Mark to malign her,
        chronicle a ruined marriage,
        your imprisonment,
        pain.

'She isn't the sort of woman you leave,' Mark says simply.

'Well, he's left her now,' I snap.
Outside, the butterfly still spins in the breeze.

'And she'll never have to know what happened
or how he felt. There's a blessing.'

'I suppose she could still find out.'
        I drain my glass.
        Mark lifts his chin.
'No, she won't, so don't even think about it.'

The table next to us fills with a loud group.
'My round,' I say, and leave him to worry,
forgetting he isn't you
and doesn't deserve to be terrorised.

I thought Mark would be enough.
        But I need more.

I want him to tell me you loathed Rebecca.
I want him to tell me our love shattered you.
I want him to tell me that if you were alive
        you would have picked me
        eventually.

When I return to the table I set down the drinks.
'Tell me I exist,' I say.

☙

Paul sends a message:
        Get milk.
But all the organic semi-skimmed has sold out.
They have full-fat organic, blue-top,

regular semi-skimmed, green-top.
I approach a shelf-stacker.
'Could you look in the back to
see if you've any green-top organic?'

She bites her pierced lip.
'Cow udders are filled with pus.
It gets infected from over-production.
Makes no difference what you buy.'

She is right: choice is a myth.
What's written on a label
is rarely what's inside.

'I'd like you to look. In any case.'

She returns with a bottle of organic green-top.
I put it into my basket,
                              head to the end of the aisle for cereal.

Paul opens the milk for tea.
'Hard day?' He eyes a hole in the
                    toe of my sock.

'Uh huh.' I search for my slippers.
I am glad to be so unsexy.
I would hate to be wanted.

∾

I was eleven and Nora was fourteen when she said,
                    'You were an accident.
                    Mum didn't want you.'
I wouldn't believe her.
We were sitting on the wall
behind our house,
legs scratching against the brickwork,
chucking raisins at pigeons.
We were still in our velvet Irish dancing dresses,
            heavy shoes,
            feet dangling limply.
Nora had won three trophies and several medals that morning
            at a feis in South London.
I hadn't placed in any dance –
            my sister was the star.

Inside, Mum and Dad were watching TV in separate rooms.
My friends were jealous we had two televisions
but I never explained why,
just made out we had money,
when anyone with eyes could've seen the state of the place.
Nora continued:
                    'You don't look like dad.'

I'd only recently learned about sex,
            what happens to bring about babies.
In biology I'd asked, 'But how do they get inside?'

The teacher sidled up to me.
        'How do they get in there?
        Don't you have any friends, Ana Kelly?'
Everyone on my bench laughed.
I pushed my little finger into the gas tap.
Behind me, in a tank, the fish stank.
Nora explained on the walk home.
        It sounded like an ugly operation.

        'I'm not saying you're illegitimate.
        But it's possible.'
She twisted my arm until it burned
and hopped down from the wall.
        'But it would explain why I'm pretty
        and you're plain.'

That night Mum gave us Rice Krispies for dinner
and tried to pretend it was a treat.

Dad did a bunk and got home three days later
        wearing new trainers.

I can't remember our curtains ever being open.

❧

The first time
we made love
we knew
that's what it was
before we'd taken off our coats.
The possibility of
turning it into
a one-night stand
never stood a chance.

We agreed to meet far from North London
at Paddington train station,
then went for tea,
and there was a second kiss.
            And a hotel.
                  And.

We planned that first time
without admitting to it
and when it came
we both knew:
there could be
no simple full stop.

ॐ

You read Raymond Carver aloud
while I made instant coffee – all the hotel had,
          plus long-life milk.
'Do you read to Rebecca?'

You sniggered and it pleased me.
'Rebecca reads to Rebecca.'

'But she reads to the boys? She must.'
          I longed to hear how she failed.

'She used to when they were little.
Less so now, you know.'

I nodded but made a sound that was disapproval.

'What's Rebecca like?'
I studied your expression.
Was I permitted to talk about her?
We rarely mentioned our spouses
despite describing every other trifle of our lives.

'Rebecca is smart and busy and a vegetarian.'

'Why did you marry her?'
I was pushing, poking,
assessing how easily that bond could bruise.
          I hoped you would admit it was doomed.

You reached for a pillow and sat up

                                    against it.

'Sometimes I think Rebecca chose me as a husband
before she chose me as a boyfriend.
Does that make sense?
I mean. I had the hallmarks of husband.
Good education. Decent family. Tall.
I hate to boast but I'm over six foot,
which women love, apparently.
And then there are my guns.'

        I grabbed the Carver and threw it at you.

'Once we were a couple,
Rebecca moulded me into a person she could love.
She had me listen to her music and read certain books.
She taught me to cook.
I was a lump of stupid clay when we met.
She turned me into something.'

This portrait was meant to tell me
everything I needed to know about Rebecca –
        how cold and controlling she was,
          how caged you'd been from the beginning.

But you curated this Rebecca especially for me.

I walked the line myself:
        Paul was homely, a planner, compassionate.
        I'd had other offers but he beat off the competition.

Now, the connection was missing,
he'd stopped listening.

I am prized – steal me.
I am desolate – save me.

What we told and what we hid.
In the end I believed myself.
But I never believed you.

'Do you like Raymond Carver?' you asked,
picking him up from the floor.

I shrugged. 'I've never been much of a short story fan.'

∾

I stuck to Tanya at university,
    chose courses she approved of,
    hung out with her hockey friends,
    shared bottles of Smirnoff Ice with her until we puked.

And I still stick to her,
joined the company when she said I should,
and now
    creep out for lunch at eleven thirty
    to help her hangover.

At the sandwich counter
my phone vibrates. It is Mark. Hope you're OK.

Tanya pays for soups and salad.
She has been watching.
'You're smiling and texting.
Please don't have an affair.
It would be so much hassle.
And I wouldn't represent you for free in a divorce.
Time is money, bitch.
Plus, Paul's a babe.'

'He's sensible and disapproving.'

'Which is why you're so well suited.'

Tanya wears fishnets with stilettos.
She sleeps with men on the first date.
Her mother is a lesbian activist.
Her father is a reclusive potter.

But when it comes to me she is conservative.
'You're the good one,' she told me at Bristol.
'Let me be bad for both of us.'

∾

I had a boyfriend from Puerto Buenos
with zits and a Rolex
who called Tanya the 'fiery one'.

He sizzled when he talked about her,
dry-humping me in his room.
Whenever Tanya showed up
he unhooked me,
stood taller,
spoke louder,
seemed to become someone.

I couldn't do that to him, to anyone –
light them up,
expose their strengths.

Engineering.
That was what he was studying.
Engineering. His father owned a company.

Tanya was dressed as Boy George
when she kissed my Spanish boyfriend.
His name? Mateo maybe.
He wore a lot of merino wool –
jumpers tied around his neck.
It was a Halloween party.
He was dressed as a pirate,
I was his parrot –
squawk squawk, all night long.
It was a funny joke,
except it wasn't funny
when I caught him and Tanya

laughing and squawk-squawking in a corner,
the point of his sword against her leg.

Tanya never apologised.
She was 1980s Boy George, a cross-dressing superstar,
I was a parrot with orange feet:

                                            squawk squawk.

Mateo melted away, disappearing altogether
along with the other Erasmus students over Christmas.

Tanya said, 'Remember that Italian bloke?
He had such bad skin.
Fuck, Ana. I don't know how you could have kissed him.'

                              ∾

I've met Rebecca before.
Yes, but that was before.

And here she is again,
   your no-longer wife,
a widow in sensible shoes,
a briefcase balanced on her knee.
'Ms Taylor, hello.' I hold out my hand.
Her grip is weak.
I am firm. 'Do come in.'

I have ordered not just tea and coffee for the meeting,
but pastries too,
and grapes,
beads of water clinging to them.
'I'm not sure you'll recall, but we've met,' I say.
'A few years ago now at the Bald Faced Stag.
Your husband was there.'
Rebecca's gaze has no destination.
Her eyes trip around the room,
        books, pictures, grapes.

'Connor dealt with the financials so … '
She waves away the notion of knowing
how to behave.
            On her left hand, a wedding band.

We begin. First, your funeral.
'It was beautiful,' she says.
It was not, I don't say.
'I'm sure. Well, that's the first claim against the estate.'

Rebecca accepts a tea and a Danish pastry,
making notes in a Moleskin of everything
she has to do:
        inform the bank, the doctor, the tax man,
        the pension scheme, the council;
        find out everything she can about your savings,
        shares, insurance, trusts.

'Can't you do any of that?'
Her tone is changed, like I am now the hired help.
        A darkness within me flexes.
I sit back, willing her to continue,
reveal the woman she is.
        Your body repulsed him, I want to tell her.
        He couldn't stand your smell.
        The colour of your flesh.

'My understanding was that the executor does it.
Isn't that what the fee is for?'
The pastry has left a jammy stain on her cardigan cuff.
She uses a fingernail to scratch at it.
I offer a napkin.

'We can do as little or as much as you like.
I'm here to make the probate process easier
and for this to get settled quickly.
Six months to a year is usual.
Shall we divide some of the tasks?'

I do not see grief in Rebecca's reluctant agreement:
        she is impatient,
        like dealing with her husband's wishes,
        his life,
        his death,
        were nothing more than a chore
        instead of a fucking privilege.

Rebecca reaches for a biro from the stack
at the centre of the conference table.
Her hands are lined,
          nine years more living than mine.
                    I never understood why you chose
                    a woman older than you.
'I'm so disorganised,' she says.
She bites her knuckles,
fearing being sent home alone with
          responsibilities and paperwork.
You did everything:
paid her parking tickets,
          called the dentist when her crown fell out.

'I'll send minutes of what we discuss in an email.
Would that help?'

She doesn't answer.
Her eyes well with tears.
I want to ask why.
          You're not crying about Connor, surely?
          He said you didn't love him.
          Tell me he was right.
          Tell me how horrendous it was.

But you also said she couldn't tell the time,
          was often late;

yet she showed up here early –
            sat waiting for ten minutes.

'It's difficult,' I say.

'You have no idea, Ms Kelly.' She clicks the biro.
'No one has a clue what I'm going through.'

                        ∽

Rebecca was a figure
who stood between us.

But what if that wasn't true?

What if you,
                after all,
were the figure
standing between
Rebecca and me?

PART TWO

Your phone rang as the food came.
I didn't notice either immediately,
too busy keeping tabs on the neighbouring couple,
making peevish assumptions
about their linked hands beneath the table,
            his furtive glances at the door.

I couldn't make out what Rebecca was saying,
but knew as you set down your chopsticks
                    you'd been summoned.
'She's crashed the car.'
My instinct was to remind you of her life insurance;
I'd advised on the policy.

I said, 'Oh, God, is she OK?'

I'd ordered sashimi as you had
when I actually preferred raw fish with rice,
a swell of soy sauce.
I studied the slabs of tuna,
looked around for a waiter.

'She's late for something.
I have to sit with the car
until the breakdown gets there.'

For a strong-limbed woman,
Rebecca found adulthood quite burdensome;
if she'd not interrupted our lunch

this incompetence would have pleased me.
'I'll pay for this,' you said.
I didn't argue,
opened up a book
so I wouldn't look
completely stood up.

Traffic burped along Whetstone High Road.
A pan of noodles screeched in the kitchen.
You lay down two twenties and said,
'We have something special, Ana.'

'We ... as in you and Rebecca, or as in ... ?'
I popped edamame into my mouth.
Too much salt.

'Give me a break.
She's late. It's not a big ask.
I'd rather be here.'

'You are here.
And now you're leaving,' I said,
forever the lawyer.

The couple next to us fell silent,
watched you struggle into your blazer
then kissed one another
quite openly,
                gloatingly,
before blowing into bowls of miso soup.

I pretended to read.
One page.
Another.
Then I ordered some salmon nigiri
with no wasabi.
The waiter rolled his eyes; he wanted the table.
I pretended to read.
One page.
Another.

But for the next hour I thought only about what you'd said –
you and me:
     Something Special.

        ᘇ

'Make him leave,' she pleads.

This woman is Tanya's client
but mentioned changing her will
    when she called,
so I am sitting in.
'If he's dangerous, you could get a court order
to have him removed,' Tanya says.

The woman is leaning in,
    hands clutching the edge of Tanya's desk.
    I am entranced by her crimped pearl roots,
    confused.

Why hasn't she taken the trouble to dye them
when the rest of her is so perfectly put together?

'He doesn't hit me,' she says.

I want to listen, but her lazy grey hair is distracting
and I wonder how much longer my feet
can go without a pedicure – I can't show
the world my toes,
though I suppose
had you been alive
I'd have painted them weeks ago.
You liked my toes,
used to put your tongue between them.

'He hides,
          jumps out,' the woman is saying.
'BOO! he shouts.
He thinks it's hilarious.
We live on a quiet lane.
I worry about killers anyway.
Once he lay on the kitchen floor
pretending to be dead.
I dialled 999. My son was at home.
When I came back into the room,
they were chopping almonds.'

'What for?'

'What?'

'What did the almonds have to do with it?'
Tanya is hiding a smirk. I can tell.
But the woman is lucid.

'Nothing. Nothing.
For God's sake, I need him to leave.
My first husband bought the house,
so it's mine,
not his.
He's my second,
         you see,
and I don't want him any more.'

'That isn't how it works,' Tanya explains.
'If he won't agree to go, it's a challenge.'

'How many people need to agree
for this sort of thing to come to an end?'
              She is earnest.
              It is a real question.

'One,' I say. 'It takes just one person to end a marriage.'

Tanya chinks her rings against her coffee mug.
She expected this to be more fun.
It usually is when we see clients together.

'You'll have to excuse me,' I say.
'My next appointment is due.
But of course
　　　　　we'll help you.'

＠

In bed you kissed my arm and I said,
'I've never telephoned your home.
But I have the number
and if I wanted to
I could call
Rebecca
and I could
destroy her.
Do you ever
think about
that?'

You kissed me again and said,
'No. No, I never think about that.'

＠

I burn a roll in the toaster.
The smoke detector sounds at midnight.

Shaking a dish towel doesn't work,
but rather than try anything else
I stand beneath the alarm
just hoping.

Paul scampers in,
        steps on to a chair and removes the battery.
'What the hell,' he mutters.

'I was hungry,' I explain.
I am still in my suit.

Paul is wearing only his underpants.
'Are you hungry?' I ask.

The butter from the fridge is too hard to spread.
I'll have to use margarine.

When I look around he is gone.
The smoke detector is exposed.

∾

Two years ago I gave your messages their own ringtone,
so I am
never
        lured into imagining
        you have contacted me from your coffin.

It is only my mother encouraging me to
                              Eat Something.

ॐ

We watched *Stranger Things* in tandem on Netflix,
          one episode per week,
dissected the retro paranormal
while we walked hand-in-hand across Parliament Hill,
          far enough from home not to feel too nervous.
But at week four,
it was evident you'd gone ahead,
                    watched
                    to the end
                    without me.
'When did you finish it?' I asked,
inviting humiliation.

          Because we had agreed.
          I mean,
          we had agreed to follow
          along together.
          For fun.

'Rebecca was in the sitting room,' you said.
'I couldn't very well ask her to get out.
Anyway, she checks her phone
through the whole thing.'

You did this a lot:
            ensured I understood
that whatever you shared with Rebecca
was spoiled by who she was
            and what she wasn't.
It was a gift – slim compensation.

'So she finished it before I did?' I asked stupidly,
speaking into a paper cup.
            And with you.
            Sitting on a sofa.
                        The same sofa?
            Of course.
            Of course you sat on
            the same
            sofa.
With mugs of tea, bare feet,
            low lighting,
            drawn curtains.
Whose job was it to draw them?
Whose to shut out the lamps before bed?

Week one Paul had asked what I was watching.
'Nothing,' I'd said, shutting him out,
switching off the TV as he sat down.
It was our show. One for us alone.

The rain came
and we gambolled down to Gospel Oak,
sheltering in a pub.
On the walls were vintage tennis rackets,
snowshoes, a rowing oar.
I reached up,
                    touched the blade of an old ice skate.
You downed half a pint within seconds.
'What's going on between us?' I asked.

You reached for my free hand.
'Well, we're best pals mostly.
And the rest too. Which is incredible.'

The rest?
Did you mean the way you folded my clothes
after we made love,
while I was in the bathroom,
            laying everything across the back of a chair
so I didn't have to scramble about on the floor
like a whore,
looking for my lost, damp knickers?

With Rebecca you had easy domesticity,
                    bedsocks and dishwashers,
something that would have seemed
like a very strange thing
for us.

❧

Graham comes in without knocking.
I am alone in the office.
Sometimes I think we should install panic buttons.
'Stop telling Helen she can slack off.
She left at four. She's paid until five thirty
and she isn't your secretary. We share her.'

'It's seven,' I say.

'But she left. At four.'

I open a private window on my browser –
Graham probably searches for porn this way but that is not my sin.
I Google 'Mark Dahl' and click on images.
Mostly they are his illustrations:
                              magazine covers, adverts.
On his headshots I zoom in.
He has too much beard.
In some photos he is overweight.

        All I have of us is one password-protected photo,
        proof that once we pressed our faces together and smiled.
        Other than that,
        Mark is our witness.

'Ana, are you even listening?'
Graham's lunch lingers on his lapel.
He has propositioned me twice.
He has propositioned Tanya only once.

I look up.
'Why did you wait three hours to sound off?'

I search for pictures of Rebecca too.
Her chin is pointy,
her expression severe.
You chose this woman over me.
Every day you made that choice.
                    'She isn't the sort of woman you leave,'
                    Mark said.

'You need a holiday,' Graham says.
He is wearing his glasses on his head
to hide the almost baldness.
His ears could do with a shave.

'You're not my boss. You're not my dad.
Stop creeping me out.'

He clears his throat.
'Oh please. The shine came off you years ago, darling.
That isn't what this is about.
Your work is suffering.
And when that happens, we all suffer.
Take a break.
That's what I'm saying.'

He doesn't wait for a reply,
          is gone.

I Google images of myself.
My LinkedIn photo is ten years old.
I am adorned in a cheap necklace.
I seem so happy in it.
Maybe I was.
It's hard to remember.

ↄ

You decided to
                 end it.

You wanted a chance to try with Rebecca,
who'd noticed a change.
         'Try what?' I asked.
'Try to try,' you replied.
'I have to think about the boys.'

It was a telephone conversation.
You couldn't see that I was doodling
words in the margins of a letter to the taxman:
         Alone
         Alone
         Alone

I didn't argue.
I agreed it had to end eventually,
felt a bit relieved we'd escaped uncaught.

The consequences were a couple of burnt hearts,
nothing more.

That night I invited Paul to see a film.
     We shared a popcorn.
     Our hands touched in the bucket.
     He smelled good. I'd forgotten how good he could smell.
     At university he was the only boy I knew who showered daily.

The morning after, I was checking my phone every few minutes,
wondering how your doctor's appointment had gone,
imagining you and Rebecca trying to try –
     at dinner, in bed.

By day five I was weeping, angry –
     you had never loved me.
And now all I had was Paul.

Two weeks into the misery you were beaten:
     Hey. You OK?

                         Sort of. You?

     Not really. I missed out on
     Britney Spears tickets.

Britney was a running joke –
     everything naughty
     eliciting an 'Oops, we did it again.'
Not funny now I think back on it.

We agreed it was unthinkable to cold-turkey it,
that we were adults and friendship was possible.
        'You're my best friend,' you said.

One week later we were in bed.

ॐ

I wore tangerine-coloured underwear
for our back-together meet-up.
You lifted my skirt slowly to reveal the gift,
and sighed as we made love,
        kissing me with so much of your mouth
mine was sore from stretching afterwards.
I said, 'So what's the plan?'

You shifted away no more than an inch.
'The plan?'

You'd written a three-page apology.
You'd said,
        I'll never not want you.
        You're my every thought.
        I'd have walked the earth for you.
Yet no plans
to make me more than your tangerine queen.

After sex we saw
The Taming of the Shrew,
barely making it to the end of another fine RSC performance
before bolting back to the hotel.

We fucked for so many hours I couldn't stay wet,
      fell asleep on my side with you in me.

In the night, mice scratched somewhere.
I made you get up to check twice.
The third time I left you in peace but
panic pounded me
and I obsessively checked Google maps for traffic.
I could have been home from Stratford-upon-Avon in two hours.
I set the alarm for six.

Next day, by the bridge,
take-away cups of tea and coffee
on the bench beside us,
we ate cream-filled doughnuts.
You claimed to hate cakes and pastries
but devoured that sweet breakfast
and licked your fingertips clean.

I saw myself reflected in your sunglasses,
did everything not to seem sad and
it worked,
      I think,

until we were standing in the road twenty minutes later
hugging out a goodbye.

My dress rose up at the back.
I worried someone would see my knickers.

'Have a good weekend, honey,' you said,
which meant:
>   *Let's not make contact until*
>   *office hours.*
Did you really believe joy was possible without you?
That being left like that on the side of a road
was a thing any person could simply accept?

All I ever wanted was for you to stay.

And sitting in the driver's seat,
I watched in the rear-view mirror
until you turned a corner,
disappeared,
and I tried
so hard
to ignore my sugar-sore teeth.

That was the first time:
trying to try.

> *I can't do this any more.*
> *We have to be realistic.*
> *What if they found out?*
> *We could call it a break –*
> > *give ourselves six months –*
>
> *see where we are.*
> *Who knows the future?*
> *Promises are pointless.*
> *You know how I feel.*

But it happened,

    again and again
    and
again and again and again.

Together

    apart.

In love

    in aching.

Tangled

    unravelling.

The pain.
The shame.
The knots
        and sleepless nights.

Again and again and again.

All the clichés.

                    ∞

The night bus jerked to a stop and I made room for
a woman with a pram, an array of
        bulging carrier bags.
She scowled at my hand
        holding the rail
too close to the face of her child.
        A child who should have been in bed.

A man nearby ate a hot Cornish pasty from a box.
The smell was sickening.

You messaged around nine,
unsympathetic to my headache
or office politics with the partners.
I've a residents' meeting, you texted.
I'm gonna have to hear about everyone's drains.

I sat on the patio with a Romanian Pinot Noir
the colour of cranberry juice,
looking through case notes.
I'd lost an important one that morning –
        a woman written out of her father's will
        when he was in sheltered care,
        her brother getting everything.
        She had a sick child.
        She could have done with a few quid.

Two yellow roses bloomed
                                at the bottom of the garden,
poking their jolly
        blonde heads out from behind the hydrangea –
                a flower never quite sure of its colour,
                lilting lavender when blue,
                and purple when pink.

You messaged once the sun had well and truly set.
They won't leave.
We're on to recycling bins.
Actually, I'm peeing.
Thinking of you and peeing.
What are you doing?
Still whinging about work?

I poured a second glass of wine,
thought of you and Rebecca
hosting your residents' meeting.

You hadn't mentioned earlier
    that it was being held in your house.
    A sort of party, really.
    Soirée.

I was meant to reply to that message,
be pleasant,
make jokes,
which you would read once the booze was gone,
the guests departed,
Rebecca safely removing her make-up,
    eyesight too blurry to see what you were up to.

It is curious,
the things you told me
and thought I would enjoy.

It is a mystery
I never chastised you for it.

Acceptance: it was my bounteous gift to you.

For a while.

            ᕬ

A parcel was couriered to my office
the day after your residents' meeting.
Inside, a sparkling bottle of Ballygowan

and a packet of fast-acting Nurofen.
You wrote a note –
wished me a less stressful day than the one before
and promised to kiss my temples better.

And you did.

You kissed my face
on a bench in Coldfall Wood
and told me you were sorry
       about the woman and her sick child,
and sorry I never had time to stop
and sorry you couldn't take care of me
and sorry you were married
and sorry I was married
and sorry also for yourself.

We didn't have long together that day.
You had a client meeting scheduled
with a television presenter
about a gaudy extension – 'a lot of glass
but not much class,'
       you said.
It was not a job you wanted
but figured it might get your
name in *Wallpaper*.
               Which it did.

We didn't have any desire to be locked in a room that day.
          It was different.
We crept through a gap in the wood's fencing
and found the older part of the cemetery,
ivy-eaten headstones, a rusting car.

'I love you,' you said.
'I love you,' I whispered.

It was the first time we had declared it.

                        ❧

I pull out the sofa bed,
curl up on the mattress without bothering to use a
sheet or find a blanket.

          Tanya got me drunk,
             promising the binge was for her benefit,
             reminding me she was thirty-seven and still single,
                two fiancés down, childless.
          'I'm rich, smart and gorgeous.
          What do men want?'
                        'Someone who isn't a cunt?' I suggested.

The mattress springs claw my back.
I message Mark.
                    Are you free soon?
He won't reply –
not when he sees what time I've sent it.

I wrap my right arm around my body,
imagine you are holding me.
I caress my left shoulder
and am kissing my hand,
desperate for warm skin and spit.
My fingers glide down my belly.

A toilet upstairs flushes.
'Mum?'
   It is Ruth.
'Mummy, are you home?'

I stay spectral.
And eventually she is silent.

∾

A pile of books
like building blocks
has toppled next to Ruth's bed –
novels,
facts,
activities.

She is wearing her school socks,
    the white soles brown.
The French plait I gave her this morning is
still in, tousled.

I place her heavy head back on to the pillow,
kiss her lips,
her breath orangey and hot.

And I am reminded of why
you could not leave.

ॐ

Jon is in bed with Paul,
horizontally lying across the end
in only a pull-up.
                His legs are splayed
                    like an open pair of scissors.
'What time is it?' Paul asks.

'You're awake,' I say.
'I'll boil the kettle.'

ॐ

I miss the way you answered my calls.
'It's you. Let me plug you in.'

And I would wait
until you found your headphones,
your voice bright when back to me.
'This is a nice surprise,' you'd say,
even if we'd only spoken an hour earlier.

I know I made you sad.

But there was joy too.
     Wasn't there?

     ᖇ

Jon squeals on the roundabout
and the roundabout squeals back.
The metal slide is scalding.
   Ruth's legs stick to it.
'Mummy, it hurts,' she shouts.

A woman slumps herself next to me on the bench,
bouncing half a loaf on her lap.
     'For the ducks,' she says,
as though I care,
as though I'm judging her for
nursing a Hovis.

The roundabout spits off a boy, who howls.
      Not Jon.

In my jeans is a twenty-pound note.
An ice-cream van idles by the exit.

I line up as Tanya appears.
She is stuffed into leather trousers and stinking of hangover.
'When do kids stop yelling?'

'I'm getting some 99s. What do you want?'

'A boyfriend who's solvent,' she says.
She ogles the weekend dads.
'And a strawberry Cornetto.'

           ॐ

I remember when I coveted noise
to cushion the guilt,
when weekends were people and people and people.
      Who could I invite?
      Where could we go?
      Fast-forward my hours away from you.

So Paul thinks it is what I want,
continues with Saturday and Sunday lunches,
friends, relatives, new potentials.
            Unless he has found someone.
            Unless he is the one doing the fast-forwarding now.

I open the oven, am attacked by heat,
roast potatoes hissing and sputtering.
The golden locket Paul bought me tips against my chest, burns.

'Maybe turn down the heat a bit,' he says. And, 'Top up?'
offering more wine, a hand grazing my elbow.

'No, thank you.'
When he is out of sight, I pour my own.
He cannot think he is winning.

Tanya says, 'You're cooking. Are you poorly?'
She speaks while checking her posture in the mirror.
She is rarely in one place.
'Remember when you boiled up vats of bulgur wheat
cos that guy – what was his name,
Turkish, wasn't he –
told you it was his favourite food?
You watered his plant over Easter,
thought it meant he loved you.
Didn't he give you a stolen hotel bathrobe to say thanks?'

'You're so good for my self-esteem, Tanya.'

'I'm the only damn person on this planet
who knows everything about you
and still loves you, Ana Kelly. Isn't that right, Paul?'

Paul is skulking,
constantly changing the music:
        nineties' pop, the Rat Pack, acoustic folk,
        The Godfather soundtrack, Ellie Goulding.
It is a form of psychological warfare:
keep everything spinning,
do not let Ana
stand still
or breathe
or notice the grain of things
                                    in silence.
If there is noise,
        she will not notice how little
        we remember one another.

Ruth appears wearing Tinkerbell wings
and a Darth Vader mask.
'You look wicked,' Tanya tells her.

She stands taller.
'I'm gonna get so many sweets at Halloween.'

'Wash your hands for lunch,' I say.
I sound like a proper parent,

someone who does this sort of thing daily,
      though I don't.
      This is Paul's domain.
        The children:
        his only chore.

The timer rings. I take out the chicken.
'I'm veggie,' Tanya says.

'Since when?'

'Since I saw that chicken.
It looks like it's about to tango out of here.'

Paul returns and reaches for the wine.
It is drained.
'Open another bottle,' I suggest.

'I'm working tomorrow,' he says.
'I'm going to take it easy.'

Tanya salutes him. 'Yes, sir.
Sorry, sir. Don't give us a detention, sir.'

He goes to the wine rack.
'I guess it's still early.'

She softens him
in a way I never manage to,
every movement of mine a mistake,
every choice, an infraction.

He skewers the chicken. The juice runs pink.
'You trying to kill us?' he asks.
He chinks glasses with Tanya. 'Cheers, Tan.'

It is as much as I can do not to skewer *him*.

ॐ

Paul opened a door for me.
He was cute: clean hair, big eyes behind round glasses,
something gormlessly Clark Kent about the way he
stepped back to let me through
and bowed his head a bit,
        dropped a book.
'What a gent,' Tanya said,
storming through before me.
She fancied everyone;
        it was sort of a joke
        and also a sickness.
Paul picked up the book.
'Maths?' I asked.
'Economics,' he said.
'First year?' I asked.

'Third,' he said. 'I stay out of the sun.'
'I worship it.'
'I've seen you at School Disco,' he said.
'I never go to those,' I replied.
School Disco was all traffic light parties
and girls in uniforms and pigtails.
Even when that sort of thing seemed tolerable,
I loathed it.

Tanya was ahead of me in the library,
putting cash on to her photocopying card
and calling, 'Lend me two quid, Ana!'

'I have two pounds,' Paul said.
He fumbled in his pockets. 'Here.'

I took the coins. It was his version of buying me a drink.
'Thanks. Maybe I'll go to School Disco.
Mondays, isn't it?'

'Wednesdays,' he said.

'Yeah, Wednesdays. I'll wear a red badge.'

'I'm amber,' he said.

Tanya shouted, 'Hurry up!'

Paul liked Tanya even then.

He thought she was the shark
that made me seem a mermaid.
No one had described me that way before
or compared me to Tanya
and held me up as the winner.

I gave Tanya the coins.
'Please don't shag that bloke,' she said.
'He's soft-core Dungeons and Dragons by day
and hard-core dungeons and porno by night.'

'And he sounds like he's from Birmingham.'
'Oh, Ana.'
'Yeah.'

When I turned he was chatting with a spectacled girl
at the library door.
Was she his girlfriend?
I didn't care.
I was better-looking.

༄

'Aren't you freezing?' you asked.
My tights had torn so I'd taken
them off
        before we met,
            undeterred by the cold.

I kept my right leg crossed over my left
to hide the worst of the spider veins.
My legs were goosebumpy.
'Shall I pop to Boots?
Tell me what to get.'

'I'm fine. Don't be silly.'

'We can't have you icing over, my little Pingu.'

We were sharing a cheesecake,
sitting by a window for once.
You rubbed my bare thigh.
'Let me go and get you some sexy stockings at least.
Order me another flat white.'

You returned after ten minutes
with one hundred-denier tights,
the kind I'd only ever worn to school in winter.

'Put these on. Go on.'

'Are you aroused?' I asked.

'Incredibly. I'm going to buy
you a puffer jacket next week.
Make you put it on in front of me.'

In the disabled toilet I hitched up the tights,

was immediately warmer.
If Paul had been so insistent
there would have been an argument.

But you weren't Paul.

So it felt like love.

&

It felt like love too
when you compared me to Rebecca,
told me she was without ambition,
that you respected my work ethic,
        my reluctance to be 'just a stay-at-home mother'.

But when Rebecca was at home
with the kids and we were together fucking …
you benefited from her lack of drive then, didn't you?
        And benefited from my work ethic.

&

Helen comes in with photocopies.
        'Can I scoot early?'

'Check with Graham.
By the way, did you hear from Ms Taylor
about the life insurance documents?'

        She straightens her jersey dress.
        A button is missing from the bottom.
        'Can I email her tomorrow?'

'No. Call her now about the documents.'

Helen storms to the window and looks outside.
'Pete's picking me up in a few minutes.'

'Then be quick.'

'Is the smell of the sardines bothering you? Is that it?'

'What? Eat whatever the hell you like.'
Outside a pigeon is cooing, shitting on the paintwork.
The tacks were meant to stop them landing on the window ledge.

'Right. Well, in that case I'm off.
Leave a list and I'll get in early.
I'm not asking Graham. He'll say no.'

'You have to ask him.

It's your job, Helen. It's your actual job to work here.'
The pigeon pecks at holey bubbles in the concrete.
Another looks to land but is bullied away.
I should put down poison.

'I'll make a cheese wrap for tomorrow.
I'm sorry if the smell of fish is sickening.
I told Pete I'd be right down.
Don't turn into one of them.'

'I need help, Helen.'

'Tomorrow, sweetheart. You can count on me.'
She turns and leaves, quietly closing the door after her.

The pigeon flies away.

I find Rebecca's phone number
and add it to the contacts in my mobile.

∾

You had a way of pinching the bridge of your nose
when you were nervous
or lying.

Didn't Rebecca ever notice when you arrived home late,

pinching
pinching
pinching

like some secret might escape
through your nostrils?
Didn't she look across the table,
over the too-dry veggie lasagne,
and say, 'What's bothering you tonight?'

It was a Sunday.
The London Marathon was almost over,
weak-limbed novices in metal blankets
scattered all over the city – enthusiastic trauma victims.
You'd gone to support Mark,
missed him at the *Cutty Sark*, mile seven,
then at mile sixteen,
cut your losses and met me at the Pavilion Café
for a toasted ciabatta and a heated debate
on euthanasia –
                    you rallied for the life of the decrepit,
You pinched your nose and I said, 'What's happened?'

'I'm expecting a call from Donna
telling me she's a widow.'

'Huh?'

'Mark didn't train,' you explained.
'He downed an oxycodone at sunrise instead.'

The melted brie from the ciabatta burned my lips.
'It isn't that. Something's going on.'

'You had sex last night,' you said.
'Don't tell me cos I don't want to know.
But you did. And I know, so ... '

A breeze came into the café and I wished I'd worn a coat.
'What are you talking about?'

I liked this hint at jealousy,
a feeling you claimed never to own.
Your eyebrows knotted
like you were imagining.
And I allowed it – blowing on the brie
to give space to the idea.
'Why would you say that?' I asked.

'You were offline for hours.
I'm not interrogating you.
I noticed, that's all.'

'And when did you last have sex?' I asked.
I hoped you'd say three weeks earlier,
when we'd met at a Hampton Inn on the A1 for a few hours.
I had stopped sleeping with Paul.
It had been months.

'Did you have sex last night?'
You cajoled, as though we were friends,
like knowing would mean nothing.

I smiled,   leaned across the table
                     and nibbled your earlobe.
If we'd been alone I would have put my tongue
into your ear.
I wanted you. I wanted you.
'No,' I said breathily. 'Did you, my sweet?'

You pinched your nose.
'I better meet Mark.
Who runs a marathon without training?'

The breeze made the hairs on my arms rise up.
'You did, didn't you? Last night?' I asked.

'Yes,' you said. 'I did actually.'

∾

Afterwards,
were you satisfied or did you need
a second helping of her?
Was it hurried? Kind?

Every evening after that day at the Pavilion Café,
I took to my bed before ten o'clock
if I possibly could,
so I would be sleeping
if and when
you fucked your wife again.

ભ

I slept with Paul the next day to spite you,
and afterwards crept into the bathroom and
cried.

I never told you what I had done:
it was not you who felt the pain of my
betrayal.

ભ

I check your Tweets,
        replies, likes, follows,
                Facebook,
                Instagram,
last seen on WhatsApp,
        in case anything has changed.

In case this has all been
some grisly mistake.

ॐ

Your will is glowing up my screen.
The details of your life.
What to give your wife now,
how much to put into trust for the boys.
I was never added to the beneficiaries,
        not even near the end,
            because you were only pretending to have chosen me.

'I'm OK,' Rebecca says. 'It's the kids.
Jamie's fighting at school. David hardly talks.
Ned suddenly has himself a goth girlfriend.
He's fifteen for Christ's sake.
My brother's staying with us for a few days.
Man in the house. You know?'
She sighs but does not sound distressed.
She is cross, perhaps, that I have called
to hound her about insurance documents,
pension scheme papers.

'Have you considered counselling?'

'Oh, yes, I've considered it.'
Something beeps in the background.

Rebecca's shoes clack across the floor.
'Anyway, I'll keep looking.
His office is a mess. I hate
riffling through everything.
Keep coming across cards and photos.
Makes me … '
        She searches for a feeling.
        Does not grab at sadness.
'Makes me wish he'd been better organised.'

He didn't know he was leaving, I want to shout.
Instead, 'Would it save time if I came over?
I'm happy to help you look.
I've done it for other clients.
I've measured up curtains for people actually.
Ordered cosmetics.
Taken dogs to the groomers.
Kids to McDonalds.'
I try for a laugh but it gets lost in my throat.
I am wearing one of Ruth's hairbands on my wrist.
I snap it. Do it again so it hurts.
'It's an overwhelming time, Rebecca.'

Only her breathing down the line.
        Relief? Suspicion?
At last she says, 'Would you really come and help?'

I wish you had left me a relic.
Your tartan shirt.
You looked drop-dead in it with the sleeves rolled up.
'Yes. I'd be delighted to come over.'

❧

So I wouldn't be
seduced by the sound of your voice, I messaged you.
I had been jittery for days after you'd revealed you
were still sleeping with Rebecca,
         my body electric, raw.

I said,
         I can't be with you when you're sleeping with her.
         If this is all we are, I'm out.
         I have to find peace, Connor.
         I can't keep doing this.
         I want more.

You replied as I knew you would.
         OK. I love you.
         I'm sorry. I am.

I deleted your number,
made fairy cakes with the kids that evening.
Then I paid the council tax,

put the bins out and ordered some verruca socks for Ruth.
Paul kissed my cheek and said,
        'You're fit, you know that?'

∞

When everyone else was drunk
and planning a gap year after graduation,
Paul was researching ISAs and PGCEs.
He wasn't sure about teaching
but he *was* sure he didn't want to be unemployed.
'You should apply to NatWest or something.
They have graduate schemes,' Tanya said,
inhaling the last dregs of the joint I'd paid for.
We were lying on her double bed
in the flat her mother had rented
after she'd left it too late to apply for third-year halls.
        Paul was in the middle.

'You think I'd do well at interview?'
Paul gestured to his boot-cut cords
and hairy bare feet.

Tanya grimaced.
'Look, you didn't do some bullshit degree like philosophy.
You have *skills*.' She thumped her chest and they high-fived.

'I like kids. And I like long holidays,' Paul said.

Tanya stroked his arm. 'What a catch.'

'Indeed, he is,' I whispered.

Paul rolled on top of me,
theatrically kissing my face, my neck, my chest.
'Tanya's just bitter because she hasn't seen my huge cock.'

'Anyway, I'll need someone to tend to the kids
when I'm busy being important,' I said.

Paul tickled me then and I shrieked. 'Stop!'
But he wouldn't. He tickled and tickled
until I confirmed to Tanya that, yes,
his cock was truly immense.

❧

Mr Bray explains how his uncle haunts him.
The uncle,
              who left Mr Bray a house in his will,
visits nightly and
stands at the foot
of the bed, giving advice:
              where Mr Bray should watch the fireworks;
              when Mr Bray should plant a hyacinth;
              how Mr Bray can coax his wife into fellatio.
'I need a restraining order,' he says.

'But your uncle is dead,' I remind him.

Mr Bray takes out a cheque book.
'How much?' he asks.
'I'll give back every penny if I have to.'
He is waving a green pen at me.
His eyes bulge.
'I'll pay court fees, lawyers. The lot.
You were so good before, at sorting it all out. I trust you.'

'It isn't about cost,' I say, glad the office is full.
'I'm not a priest. I can't stop a haunting.'

Mr Bray sits back in the chair,
appears to say a prayer, then stands.
'I think he'll visit you from now on,' he tells me.
'I've informed him you'll be acting on my behalf.'
He starts to back out of my office.

'Where are you going?' I ask. 'Sit down.'

'Thank you so much, Ms Kelly.'

'Sit down,' I say again. 'Sit down.'
But he will not.

'Is it all meat?' I complained,
ensuring the waiter overheard.

I don't know why I whinged
or what I was expecting,
where I thought you were taking me
or even what I wanted.
  No,
    that isn't true.
I always knew
what I wanted.

You wore the tartan shirt,
seemed older,
never more attractive.
I wanted to tell you –
  wanted to say, *You look beautiful*,
but didn't.

You said,
'I've been broken without you.
Rebecca and I have argued constantly.
I stayed in a hotel for a few days.'

I waited for more, looked concerned when really
I was overjoyed.
  I hated Rebecca by then.
  I wanted her to die.
  I wanted *you* to want her to die.

'We aren't having sex, Ana.
That was one time. A weird one-off.
I have no idea why I told you.
You know that I tell lies every single day.
But I don't lie to you.
And maybe that's part of our problem.'
You had a sty,
        were struggling to see out of it.
        Still   so   beautiful.
I was glad you had called,
        summoned my return.

'I don't abstain with Paul for *you*,' I explained.
'I abstain for myself.
I don't *want* to sleep with two men.'
I cried in front of you for the first time.
Instead of reaching out, you looked into your placemat.
The waiter arrived with our drinks.

After ham hock and steak
we walked along the quayside,
slippery from noncommittal rain,
and made plans
for next time,
like the day was already done with us.

And it was.
It was done before we had parked the car.

I hated Cambridge
to the same extent you loved it.
We went so often and
      each time you pointed out your college,
         Magdalene,
like I could forget your prestigious education.

Back on the road
we didn't go through the same old stuff,
but silently held hands,
which helped with the goodbye –
      a brisk kiss by the boot
in a KFC car park
where I'd left my Nissan.

      I hurried away.
      Didn't look back.

I had decided that day to make
a point of never looking back again.

❧

Mark is smoking a cigarillo,
nipping the tip of his tongue
between thumb and forefinger
to be rid of a fleck of tobacco leaf.
He is reading *L'Étranger*

in what looks like
the original French.
'*Aujourd'hui, maman est morte*,' I say,
taking a seat opposite,
        facing the sun.

'A-level French?' he asks.

'Law with French at uni,' I tell him.
'Spent a year in Marseille.'

'Oxbridge reject?'

'Naturally.' I bow slightly.

'Connor was Cambridge.'

'He mentioned it once or twice.'

Mark closes his book, raises a finger
to call the waitress.
                I order wheat beer.

'I'm looking to illustrate it,' he says.
'Just beginning some sketches.
The beach. The funeral.'

My beer arrives with a side of salted pumpkin seeds.

The sun is in my eyes.
I shift the folding metal chair,
unbutton the top of my blouse.

Mark recommends a film,
two books,
a chain of tapas restaurants
and his optician.
He doesn't ask for advice,
even when I explain why a will would be a good idea.

'Why didn't you call to tell me Connor had been in an accident?'
I'm on my fourth drink. I wouldn't be so accusing otherwise.
      Mark isn't quite listening.
      He is looking at a girl's arse in jeggings.
      It's a nice arse. I admire it myself.
'When he got taken into hospital, you could have called.
I could have come. No one else knew to do that.
I know he gave you my number.'

He peels his eyes from the arse.
'You couldn't have come.
You couldn't have done that.'

'I was the last person he spoke to. Did you know?
I mean, probably.
Fifteen minutes before the collision.
We spoke.'

And we argued. And I held my gut and
squeezed and squeezed and squeezed.
I called you names, hated you, wished you dead.
And then.

Maybe it's true:
the universe is listening.

I propose dinner, a treat for him agreeing to meet
again,
and he nods, knows
he is doing me a kindness.

On the walk to the Moroccan place
with more outdoor seating, Mark says,
          'They have blankets if we're cold.'

'Are you cold?' I ask him, stopping,
putting my hand behind his head
and pulling him to me.
He smells of my father.
And he knew you.

'What are you doing?'
He pushes me
                    into oncoming traffic.
A scooter swerves, honks,
shouting and swearing.

'Are you insane?
You thought I was interested?
Are you actually insane?'

On the kerb I cry
and ask myself the same question.
Are you actually insane?

PART THREE

Ruth and Jon pan for gold
in a sandy man-made stream,
up to their elbows in dirty water.

Around us children scream
delightedly,
detecting fake golden nuggets in their pans.
The parents are equally cheerful.

I scan the farm for Paul,
        who is taking his time to find the toilets.
Ruth cheers, opens her palm to unveil tiny pieces of treasure.
'I got ten,' she says. 'I win a medal!'

Another mother coos as though
genuinely impressed. 'Wow! Well done!'

'Good girl. Help Jon now. He's only got two pieces,' I tell Ruth.

'It's so great here, isn't it?' the cooing mother says.
She is carrying a rucksack,
filled with sandwiches and fruit presumably,
maybe a first-aid kit.

'I prefer the pub,' I tell her.

She laughs. 'Oh, yes. We all do.'

I don't believe her. She looks like she was born
in those Sketchers.

Paul taps my shoulder.
'Shall we eat? The queues have died down.'

Ruth and Jon collect enough nuggets and we
swap them
at the gift shop for medals.

Ruth hands hers back.
'Can I keep the gold instead?'

The cashier is confused.
'The medal is a prize for finding them.
We put the gold back into the river later
for other children to find.'

'The gold is better,' she says.
'The medal is plastic.'

I do not interfere as
the cashier grudgingly hands over ten
pieces of pyrite and takes back the medal.

At lunch I tell Ruth, 'You were right to keep the gold.'

She rolls the pieces between her fingertips,
eats a butterless ham sandwich. She has my eyes.
'It wasn't a fair swap,' she says. 'It was a cheat.'

Paul showers,
leaving the door to the en suite
             open so I can't get
even
ten uninterrupted minutes
to think of you and touch myself.

He stands over me in his pants,
             drying his hair roughly.
'That guy at the school – Nonno?'

I look up from *Anna Karenina*.
'What?' I turn a page, though
I have been reading the same paragraph for two weeks.

'He's a parent in Jon's class.
Italian or Portuguese or something.'

'I've no idea what you're talking about.'

He throws the towel towards the radiator.
                    Misses.
'He's always whistling. I can't stand it.'
The towel is a wet lump on the floor –
            on the carpet.
'I don't trust him.
Pretty sure he's on his second marriage.
You see why that happened.'

'Are you going to pick that up?'

My phone bleeps.
I close my book.
A message from Mark:
            I won't be meeting you again.
            Sorry it's hard but I can't.
            You need help. Get help.

'Haven't you noticed the weird whistling?'
Paul checks his jawline in the bathroom mirror,
runs the tap for a shave.

'Please close that door,' I say.
I turn over in bed and switch out my light.
By the time he is done,
I could conceivably be asleep.

I message Mark.
What do we say
when someone tells us it's over?
There is no reply to rejection
except one word:
OK.

The clocks click back.
An hour seized for sleeping.

Time shifts.
Tick.
Tock.

If only.

I would be kinder.
I would save you.
It's a minute I need.
One.

Someone else can have the other
fifty-nine.

Give them to Rebecca.
Let Rebecca have fifty-nine minutes of you.
One for me.
One.

That last one only.

ॐ

You flew home from a funeral:
your cousin's child in County Down,
and we met in the Hilton, Stansted.

     'She was eighteen,' you said.
     'Just got a place with *Riverdance* for the summer.
     You should have seen her in her hard shoes.
     She was unreal.
     Gorgeous too.'
     You traced circles on my cheeks with your finger.
     'She was my first niece.
     I planned to leave her money in my will.
     Kim. Remember?'

'Yes. I remember.'

     'She was political too.
     Painted these huge abstract canvases in acrylics
     using green, white and gold.'

'She sounds incredible.'

'She *was* incredible.

Not that I can talk to Rebecca about all that stuff.

She finds Anglo-Irish politics tedious.

She finds me tedious most of the time.'

I smoothed stray hair from your face,
kissed your chin, your eyelids.
This was a new melancholy, not about us,
and I despised myself for enjoying it.

'I can't believe Kim's gone.
It doesn't make sense. I just … '
You stood up, stretched,
went to the bathroom to run the shower.

'Why are you washing,' I asked, 'when we haven't had sex?'

'I've been travelling,' you called out.

I lay on the bed wishing you'd hurry up,
    resentful of the minutes you were wasting
    when we could have been holding one another.

Steam wafted into the room, fogging up the full-length mirror.
Bottled water on each bedside table. Mints too.
Closed curtains the colour of nutmeg.
Cushions I'd pushed straight on to the floor.

You came back in, a towel around your waist. Hair wet.

'Are you worried my perfume's rubbed off on you? Is that it?'

You looked offended.
'I didn't notice your perfume,' you said.
'But *she* might.'

'How do you know she doesn't wear the same one?'

That day I had loved you for five hours
without once feeling spiteful or stupid or used,
and at the last moment you managed it –
                                    made me a mistress.

'I'm joking,' you said, sitting on the edge of the bed.
'You wear Jo Malone, nettle and tofu scented.
It's the best thing about you.'

'It's Peony & Blush Suede, you dickhead.'

You pressed your nose into my neck and inhaled.
'I could breathe you in forever, Ana.
I could live on this alone.'

&

I am surprised every time it hails –
the violence of frozen rain
clattering
against umbrella, roof, bonnet, door, glass –
that I occasionally mistake it for thunder.

How can little pellets sound so angry?

I   extend a palm,
          accept the sky's offering.

But they hurt,
          the hailstones on my hand.

&

In the hallway,
          a pile of trainers, football boots,
some battered books and an open, empty violin case.
'Excuse the chaos,' Rebecca says,
guiding me inside by the elbow, air kissing one cheek.

Her hair tickles my face.

My stomach is sore.

'The cleaner comes tomorrow and I hate for her to feel useless.'

She is barefoot. Her feet are narrow and pretty.

'Coffee?' she asks.

'Just some tap water.'

I took the last of my diazepam on the bus.

Still my right hand wants to shake.

I sit on a kitchen stool, on my jittery hand.

The counter is cluttered:

papers, magazines,

salt and pepper grinders,

a pestle and mortar containing paper clips and coins,

a breadboard covered in crumbs, marmalade,

                        a block of sweating cheddar.

'I have sparkling somewhere.'

She opens a cupboard, pulls out Perrier.

'Really kind of you to come, Ana.

Is it OK to call you Ana? Please call me Rebecca.

When anyone says Ms Taylor I think of my mother.

She died last year.

We had to airship her home from Spain. She was on holiday.

Gosh, I don't know why I'm telling you that.'

I already know all about her mother.

The body was bruised when they opened the casket,
knocked around in cargo,
a trickle of dried dead-woman fluid crusted beneath her nose.
She had no travel insurance.
Cost you a fortune to fly her home.
'Yes, call me Ana,' I say.
I am as prim as a primary school teacher,
flat shoes, navy trousers.
I have tissues tucked up my sleeve.

Rebecca scatters digestive biscuits on to a plate,
passes me a glass of water.

She is forty-six, rich, with incredible posture.
But she is nervous, I think, busily fussing.
Her hair is greasy. The house smells of neglect.
'I can get started straight away,' I say.

She ushers me down the hall.
On the wall is a wedding photo –
        the two of you arm in arm,
                lit up with glee.
I hesitate, touch the frame.
'I was skinny then,' Rebecca says. 'Only ever ate Ryvita.'
'You're still slim,' I say.
                Your hair is longer,
                        side-swept.
'Not like that. I used to think Kate Moss was a goddess.
Heroin chic, and all that.'

By your office,

> she balances on the threshold

and says, 'Feel free to ransack the place.
And if you come across any villainy,
I'd rather not know.
I'll get out of your way.'

She stays where she is, watching me remove my jacket,
pull my hair into a ponytail.
I am hardly able to see anything around me.
'It shouldn't take too long,' I tell her.

'I'll get out of your way,' she repeats.

∾

My briefcase conceals all the documents I need.

You were sensible enough to leave them with me.
But I needed to find a way into your home,
to study your phone bills, calendar, search for a remembrance.

> I immediately find several items to stash:
> a pen, a photograph,
> a small tube of lip salve.

But after rooting around I realise Rebecca was right –
nothing incriminating in the drawers
or the envelopes within them.

Just receipts and invoices,
birthday cards from your kids.
I am nowhere here.
                    You would not take the risk of a keepsake.

At your desk, I lay my hands on the keyboard,
run my trembling fingertips along the letters.
It is as much as I can do not to put my mouth against them,
find the lingering taste of you.

Water rattles through the pipes;
upstairs a shower fizzes to life.

I wait a moment
then go to the door, call out quietly.
'Rebecca? Rebecca?'
Nothing.
Just the hum of your house.

In the kitchen,
I run my hand across the counter, hob,
the top of the metal pedal bin,
the things you orbited every day,
owned for so long
and abandoned in death.

I click the kettle. It hisses into action.
Above, a shelf is lined with jars and pots.
I help myself to a peppermint tea,

stand at the back doors looking out,
the mug between two hands.
The patio is greenish,
weeds grow through the cracks in the slabs.
I can't imagine it was this way
when you lived here.

The kitchen smells of mould.

'I should have offered you tea. Sorry.'
I turn.
Rebecca leans against the doorframe in a dressing gown,
her wet hair in a twisted towel.

I approach her.
Without make-up, Rebecca has no eyebrows.
Her pointed chin is slightly spotty.
'No. Not at all. I better get back to it.'

'I'm glad you made yourself at home,' she says
and smiles as an afterthought.

&

She knocks before entering the office,
      like I own it now.
'I have to do the school run.
Will you be OK for twenty minutes?
Perhaps a tad longer if the boys want to stop at the bakery.'

I do not mean to lick my lips but somehow that is how I reply.
By licking my lips and nodding assent.

∾

Your bed is unmade, the duvet pushed to the end,
oversized cushions cluttering the carpet.
On one bedside table, half-empty glasses of water,
an apple core.

On your side,
a neat stack
of novels.

I find nothing you owned in the wardrobes,
just dresses, skirts, women's shoes.
Each drawer in the dresser is filled too
with Rebecca's possessions:
bras and knickers,
tights rolled into unknottable fists,
scarves for all seasons.

In the oval mirror above the dresser is a face.
It is terrified.
And it is mine.

Down the hall I discover you
in a box room along with
ski gear, wetsuits and board games.

Has this always been the way or did she move
    your things when you died to make more room for herself?
I flick through each shirt and suit,
press my nose against them, hold you.

'Just me again. Forgot some post!' Rebecca calls out.

I am still. Do not speak. Listen as she fumbles in the hall,
jangles her keys. 'Definitely going now!'
The door slams shut and I slump on to the floor,
fold myself into a ball.

Cry.

ᘏ

I find your tartan shirt, the one composed mainly of pinks,
and put it on.
Then I set a timer on my phone for five minutes,
go back to the bedroom
and lie in the space
you once filled,
with my eyes closed.

ᘏ

After four hours my fingerprints are everywhere.
Stolen trinkets are buried at the bottom of my briefcase.
'I got everything I need,' I tell Rebecca.
She is at the dining table, rearranging a
selection of fabric swatches.
'Oh good. I'm glad.'

In the sitting room your boys are
on phones or
watching TV.
They do not see me.

'I'll just pop to the loo before I go,' I say.

'Yes. It's the door next to the office.'

The bathroom is dirty –
        spat-out toothpaste stuck to the basin,
        hair on the floor.
I open the cupboard.
Inside the usual paracetamol, an aerosol air freshener, Sudocrem.
And also
a barely used bottle of Jo Malone, Peony & Blush Suede.
A gift, of course, from you to her.
        So you would not be caught.
I sit. Stare at my hands.
There is no toilet roll, just a cardboard tube.
The picture on the wall is of a little boy on a swing.

In the dining room Rebecca says,
'It's odd that Connor chose to use the firm as executor.'
She holds a floral swatch to the light.
'Is it a normal thing to do?
He'd always said Mark would do it.
His best friend.'
On the table is a cup of coffee.
I'd expected her to be on wine by noon.

> You told me Rebecca liked to drink.
> You said she polished off a bottle a night,
> > sometimes gin too, fruit-flavoured beers.
> I thought I knew her.
> I assumed she was poison.
> > I thought she would be perfect.
> > And awful.

'His friend was surprised too.
You've not met Mark, have you?'

My hand begins its twitches again.
I reach for my briefcase.
'It's something a lot of clients do
to saved loved ones from stress.
I'm sure Connor was trying to be kind.'

'Not that he cared about stressing me out when he was alive.
He was a pain in the arse.
Aren't they all?'
She laughs.
I laugh.

154

But the room is filled with grief.
A timer beeps.
Rebecca jumps up.

'I'll let myself out,' I say. 'And I'll be in touch.'

'You are wonderful. Thank you.'

She turns and almost skips away.
On the hall table are a pair of blue gloves.
I slip them into my briefcase.
Can add them to my collection.

∾

I'd seen a photo on your phone so already knew
Rebecca owned a pair of
royal blue
leather gloves.
I hated her for it –
discovering she had
the nerve for such a statement,
an extravagance.

It was hard to know
whether or not a brown pair, unlined,
could compare,
but I bought them in the January sale

from Selfridges
and hid them in a drawer,
to wear with you
when it was cold.

I never found the courage.

And I never found out whether or not
the way to win you was
to be different to Rebecca,
to be better than her
or simply
          to be her completely.

Dad didn't like holding hands unless I was wearing gloves.
On the rare days he walked Nora and me to school
we wore a glove each, even in the summer,
so he wouldn't have to touch us.
Mum said he'd been that way with her too.
'He didn't like holding your hand?' I asked.

'He wasn't a big man for human contact.'

I knew this. I had seen it.

The way Dad slid by her in the kitchen, turning himself into a slice.
How he held keys from the ring and dropped them into her hand.

'I don't know why you put up with his shit,' Nora said.
We were in the park with the kids and her two Labradors
while her husband, Phil, was at the rugby.

Mum took Nora's hand and kissed it.
'But just look what he gave me,' she said.
I walked on ahead.
I didn't want Mum's spit on my skin.

&

No matter how I reprimand her,
Tanya continues to turn up with Haribo.
Paul gives me an impatient eye and says,
            'Before you head out, I'll nip to Tesco
            for a few cans.
            Single dad's night in.
            Just me and the football.'

Tanya and Jon build a Lego Star Wars spaceship
on the rug.
            Ruth watches Netflix on Tanya's phone.

I find a fresh shirt.
Change my socks.

Tanya uses the toilet,
accepts a mug of tea,
then a second.

The sun sets.
Tanya never checks her watch.
She offers to build a jigsaw.
I replace the light bulb in the downstairs loo
and order groceries to be delivered tomorrow.

'Where's Daddy been?' Ruth wants to know
as he pulls up on to the kerb outside.
He has Chinese takeaway in one hand,
two Tesco carriers in the other.

'You should go.'
He smiles.

'We've missed the beginning,' I murmur.
In the kitchen
Paul upends the shopping:
salami,
oranges,
muffins.
'There'll be adverts.
Hurry and you'll catch it.'

'We've missed the film,' I tell no one.

Ruth is practising gymnastics in the hallway –
        cartwheels, bridges.
'Stop that!' I scream.
'You'll smash your head against a radiator
and we'll be in A&E all night.'

Paul holds an inky avocado in his left hand
and
        without looking at me
squeezes.
        Squeezes
        until there is creamed avocado
        between his fingers.

Tanya is sporting a tiara.
'Pub?' she asks brightly.

Paul murmurs behind clenched teeth then turns,
washes his hands in the sink.
I am sick in my mouth, swallow it back down.

'Let's go round the corner for a Guinness,' Tanya continues.
She leads me out by the hem of my jacket.

I say nothing until
we are pushing open the doors of The Starting Gate.

And what I say is,
'I loved someone and now he's dead.
I don't know what to do, Tanya.'

She pats my hand.
'He's in there somewhere.
Marriage just messes everything up.
I could have told you that twenty years ago.'

༄

After uni Tanya and I lived together
in Kentish Town,
in another flat that belonged to her mother.
It was a one bed with William Morris wallpaper in every room.
        I was to pretend I didn't live there,
        my rent paying half of Tanya's,
        her mother feeling wise and responsible
        for insisting her daughter fend for herself.
I slept on the sofa,
kept my clothes in the sideboard
next to the gin and coasters.

I stayed hidden.
It was good practice.

༄

I helped you choose a pair of shoes for a wedding.
An emoji thumbs up
              or down
to pictures sent
of smart lace-ups, shiny loafers.

Yet you went to the wedding with Rebecca –
posed for a photo I saw
when I stalked you on Facebook
        then couldn't shut out,
your arm draped around her,
fingers firmly pressed into her upper arm.

Rebecca wore a sleeveless dress,
her make-up obviously applied
by a professional – feline eyes.
She was unbearably elegant,
gazing into the camera
with the confidence of someone
long established.
            I am the wife.

In your free hand, a green beer bottle,
        part of the label
        peeling away,
        curling around your thumb.

Her shoes were silver, high,
too many straps.
Impractical for dancing.

I have nothing which proves we ever were.

I would have danced.

༄

I imagined you writing a list –
       pros and cons
       me and her
       for and against
       good and bad
       stay or go
wondering how I measured up
and
knowing I was always the loser.

༄

I swivel in the chair, show the hairdresser a picture.
'I'd love to go with something like this.'

Katie, her own hair tied into an untidy topknot,
dressed in all black – regulation senior stylist –
       assesses me in the mirror.
'Sure you wanna go that short?
People usually cut it in stages.'

'I don't need it,' I say.

I have had long hair my whole life,
        never risking the shock of a drastic change.
I have dyed it auburn since Bristol.
I have been the same person on the outside
            always,
while in me
another person grew.

    When you came along I panicked at the thought of
    making even moderate alterations –
    what if you hated short hair, long nails, Nike trainers?
    I stayed still in time.

'So long as you don't cry once I've done it.'
She unties her own hair and it falls down
her back like a tease.
'Tea or coffee?'
She hands me a copy of *Hello*.
Nora's friend Allie dated a rock star for a while,
very married,
            definitely leaving,
    and she trusted him until,
            at the hairdressers for a blow-dry,
    she saw a photo shoot of him
in a magazine, posing with his wife on a beach in Bermuda.
    The wife was pregnant.
    Glowing.

Katie brings a coffee.
'Plans for the weekend?'

I open the magazine. 'My boyfriend's taking me away.
Don't tell my husband.'

She laughs.
'What happens in the chair stays in the chair.'

'The new style will remind him of his wife.'
I open *Hello* and let her get on with it.

        She doesn't ask any more questions.

              ∾

When you buy a rabbit,
they never tell you
what to do once the thing
stops eating and drinking,
hardly moves any more
and looks at you with agony eyes
as though you're some sort of animal God who could
breathe new breath into its rattling throat.
'It isn't kind to keep her alive.

I'll take her to the vet,' Paul says,
	stowing Jump
	in a cardboard box with some straw.
	Ruth is already crying.
	Jon says, 'Can we get a puppy?'

'Why don't we wait and see how she is later?' I suggest.
'It's a bit macabre to do it on Halloween.'

The kids survey Paul.
Ruth says, 'I love her.'
She puts her hand into the box but is bitten, screams.
'What's wrong with her?'

'She's dying,' Paul says gently.
Ruth runs out of the room.
Jon follows, yapping like a dog.

'Don't put her down,' I plead.

'For Christ's sake, Ana,
are you trying to upset everyone?'

'Why can't you be kind to me?'
I am crying too now.
I do not want anything killed.

'To be honest, Ana, you don't really
respond all that well to love.'
He pets the rabbit. She is completely still.
'I'll be back soon,' he says.

And he is.
Back within a couple of hours, the box still in his hands.
Jump is nibbling on a radish but looks much smaller,
fluffier.
'Miraculous recovery,' he tells the kids,
eyeing me a warning stare.

They are pleased.

∾

I wanted to brush the ears of
a blue roan cocker spaniel
on long evenings,
have something to welcome me home
with unabashed excitement.

I would have trained it to sleep
in the kitchen at night,
never nip strangers or
piss in the herb garden.

But you hated pets:
their fur, breath, friendliness.
And so I never got a gun dog.

I didn't want to have to give it up once you and I
found our way to one another.

I couldn't give you another excuse

to stay away.

My Polish neighbour,
the nurse on early mornings
with a delicately boned face
and a loud alarm,
is hanging laundry.
I saw her from Ruth's window
and dashed down
two stairs at a time
with some already-dry shirts.
'Hey,' I say
through chicken-wire fencing
and a holly bush.

'Hello,' she says.

'How are you?'

'Good. You?'

'Yes,' I say. 'Good.
Mother's chores are infinite.'
I have never cared
enough to ask her name
and realise it's a bit late now.
'You're in medicine, aren't you?'

'I'm a nurse.'

'Ah, yes. At the Whittington?'

'Yes.'

'I should go to A&E later.
My neck is so sore.
I'm in agony actually.'

I cannot see her expression.
Slowly, she pegs a tea towel to the line.
'Yes, you can do that.
Or take ibuprofen
and call your GP tomorrow maybe.'

'No good asking you for drugs then?'
I laugh. It's worth a try.

Painkillers and a cold gin
would take the edge off.
I could make lunch
and iron the uniforms,
face a family film at the Odeon later.

She mostly has her back to me.
'Hope you feel better,' she says. 'Bye-bye.'

Next time I will remember to ask for her name.

༄

I hardly heard from you when you holidayed in Corsica.
        It was the second year of us;
        we were calling every day,
        meeting weekly.
'WiFi was awful,' you said on your return.
'And I couldn't get a second to myself.'
You knew I didn't believe you.
You'd read three books
and contacted your junior architects.

Each one of those ten days,
seven,
four,
one,
was a test,
imagining

sunscreen oozing between Rebecca's fingers
as she lathered your back
to prevent melanoma stealing you away,
                    not knowing you'd be taken anyway.
                    So quickly.
                    No warning.
                              Gone.

Nights were worst.
Time for bed,
bodies lying close in the dark,
feet touching.
How often did you resist her?
'Always,' you said.

I pictured it all:
            the colour of the sun loungers,
            the other hotel guests.

I waited for my phone to ping,
to know I hadn't been obliterated entirely.

                    ෨

I went on holiday too.
                    Lanzarote. Lisbon. Skegness.
But I phoned you, didn't I?
I waited for Paul to slide into the pool

or to take the kids to the toilet.
I said, 'I just wanted to hear your voice.'

'I miss you,' you replied.

I never set you aside or tried to torture you.
I never made you invisible.

ॐ

Tanya strides into my office.
'You know when we forged sick notes for PE?
Well, would it be terrible to do that now?'

'To forge a doctor's sick note, you mean?
Do you need time off?'

She rolls her eyes. 'Would *you* ever sign something
on behalf of someone else?'

'With no power of attorney? What's going on?'
I glance behind her at the open door
and wonder if she's about to confront me.

'Passport form,' she says. 'I don't think it's terrible.'

I unclench my jaw.
'Can you get caught? You might.
You're not as smart as I am.'

'I am prettier though. Since you hacked off all your hair.
    You look like Annie Lennox, you know.
    And Annie Lennox looks like a dog breeder.'

'Bring it in here, and I'll sign it,' I say.

'You already did. That was what I meant.'
She flounces out. 'Thanks, babes!'

'Utterly pointless forgery.
You'll get debarred!' I shout.

'Don't worry, Orphan Annie, I'll say I sought legal counsel!'

❧

You called me Rebecca once,
                    by mistake,
and it would have felt like a punch
but as we were in the middle of an argument,
it was actually OK.

❧

'My hands might be cold,' Dr Myers says,
making me stand,
            bend,
                stretch,

172

pressing her fingers against my skin,
prodding the pebbly discs in my spine.

I gasp – a show of bravery – shut my eyes.
'I go to the gym a couple of times a week,' I lie.

She scrolls through my history.
'You're on citalopram,' she says,
      her voice even.

I straighten my skirt,
      tuck my vest back into it.

'How's that working for you?'
Her eyes stay fixed to the screen.

'Fine,' I say.
'Well, I could probably do with a higher dosage.
Maybe something else for panic attacks.'

'Right.'
Her desk is piled high with paper of assorted colours.
She is wearing too many rings for a woman
      with a good education.
Her forehead is full of Botox.

Dr Myers is older than I am and
I could tell her everything, I think, and she would not blink.
'You're a teacher,' she says,
glancing at the scuffed toes of my shoes.

I nod, I don't know why,
          and allow one corner of my mouth to curl,
a gesture that lets her feel she's read me,
seen what all this neck pain is about:
          work, an abysmal state system.

'Half-term soon,' I say,
wondering if Paul will expect me to take time off
when there's no need – he'll be off anyway.

'Don't remind me. Thank God for kids' clubs.'
She clicks her mouse,
                              once, twice.
'You need to keep up with the gym, which
will help your mood, and pain relief.'

'Of course.' I wince lightly,
hoping I'm not overplaying it.

                    Sometimes I ache for you.
                    But otherwise my body is fine.
                    It is my head that needs these drugs.

'I've started fencing,' I say.
I have always wanted to try it,
and I might, now I've said it.

'I'm prescribing painkillers.
Stronger than over-the-counter.
Only take them as needed,
and come back if
you get further numbness in your arm.'

I hold on to the printed prescription without
thanking her.
Gratitude would imply it was what I'd come for.

'And I need more of my pill,' I tell her.

'Ah, yes, right,' she says, squinting at the screen
then up at the wall clock.
'Give me two secs.'

Outside the air is musty and uneven.
A cat is pissing next to the wheel of my car.

&

'I never intentionally hurt you,' you said.

We were hunched near a man-made lake in Milton Keynes,
had spent sixteen satisfied hours together
        and now this,
        a performance I could have predicted,
                could not have prevented.

Do not be cruel, I told myself.
I told myself, *Be reasonable. Be charming.*
'Really?
Remember when you admitted you'd fucked Rebecca?
Did you forget that?
Telling me, I mean.
Not the actual fucking.
You'd recall doing that.
You're just back from a cosy family holiday
        so fresh memories too maybe.
Call of duty and all that.
Wine helps, I find,
though children
are a hindrance.'

Your right fingers flinched
like you might have had it in you to hit me.
Honestly, it would have been a comfort.

'I'm sick of this, Ana.
Every time.
Every single time.
Why can't we just enjoy one another?'
You walked to the water's edge
                and back again.
A swan bobbed up from between tall reeds,
honked and flapped.
'I love you. Isn't that enough?'

My high-heeled boots
       sank into the sludge of soil and goose shit.
'No.'

I wanted you to tear
the world to shreds
         to get
         to me.

         I wanted to be chosen.

It was the first time I screamed.
Into the clouds, sending the swan for cover.
'I can't do this any more,' I cried.
'You love me, but it's her name on the certificate.
Please help me. Tell me what to do.
I can't carry on like this.'

'And I can't make your choices for you, Ana.'

'Tell me what to do.
You or not you.
Stay or go.
Tell me.
Tell me.'

You pulled me into your shoulder.
I coughed and snotted on your shirt.
'It's eleven o'clock. We better check out.'

I tried to keep hold of your hand
when you shifted gears on the way home,
but it was impossible not to let go occasionally.

Paul said, 'How was the conference?'

'It gave me a migraine,' I said,
and tossed my soiled clothes into the washing machine.

∾

'I need new hiking boots,' I say,
holding my old ones aloft,
knocking their soles together,
the mud cracking,
            peppering the floorboards.

'I'll order you a pair,' Paul says.
He has just finished a pile of marking,
is on his way out to the carwash,
has agreed to take the kids for pancakes too,
so I can catch up with housework.

'I'd like to choose my own,' I tell him,
adding the boots to a bag for Oxfam,
along with some unused barbecue tongs
and a Barbie doll with Sharpie scribbles
along her limbs.

He is wearing straight-cut jeans.
His hair is growing too long.
I am not sure why he needs to dress so much like his dad.

I reach for the mop
but spend the free hours idle
on the couch.

When Paul arrives home he hands me a box –
       inside
a pair of high-end hiking boots
with clean pink soles.
Their newness squeaks.
'Ten per cent off,' Paul says,
watching me slot them back into place,
cocooning them in crackling paper.

'What's wrong?' Paul asks.
The children are behind him, waiting.
It was a surprise.
I am meant to be smiling.

'Nothing, they're nice.'

I'd jumped up to make stew as they arrived
so go back to chopping onions.

In bed he says, 'Lovely grub earlier, thanks.'

'Don't patronise me, Paul,' I say.
He switches off the light and turns over,
too bored to look at me.

'I'm happy to have an argument, Ana.
But I'm on a trip tomorrow so I need some sleep.
You mull over exactly what I've done wrong now
and email me.
I assume you won't be home early enough
tomorrow to have a real conversation
or feed the kids or help with their homework.
Sound good?'

'Feed the kids with the food *I* shopped for, you mean?
With the food taken from the fridge *I* clear out every week
and cooked in the oven *I* clean?
Sure, I'll email you.'

I want to tell him
about us, you,
shock him into giving a shit.

I look at rentals on my phone,
weigh up the idea of leaving,
and wish to Christ I was a better person.

ॐ

You read *Wills, Probate & Inheritance Tax for Dummies*
        so you could listen
to me talk about my work and understand.

At the time it seemed a strange thing to do –
        a way of having opinions,
                                typical man –
        and I was threatened.

Looking back,
I must remember
you are not Paul.

℘

'Can I have Ready Brek?' Jon asks.

I have fried bacon.
I have warmed a frozen baguette.
The clementines are peeled
and placed in Tupperware for break time.
The kitchen reeks of good parenting.

'You can have what I've made,' I say,
        presenting him with breakfast.

'But I want Ready Brek.'

'No,' I tell him,
because the dregs
will dry against the bowl like concrete
and I will have to scrape them away with my nails.

Jon starts to cry.
'Can he have a cheese string then?' Ruth wonders aloud.
For siblings they are unnaturally kind to one another
and I don't like it, this army of two,
the odd habit they have of holding hands
around other people,
          wanting to sit next to one another,
          sharing desserts with absolute fairness.

'He can have bacon and a roll.
He can have bacon *or* a roll.
Alternatively, he can have nothing.'

Jon cries harder.
Paul comes into the kitchen looking fresh.
He has an interview for a deputy headship.
'What's wrong, mate?'
He leans in to his son, away from me.

'I've made hot breakfast and it's a fucking Tuesday.
He's having what he's given.'

'I usually make Ready Brek,' Paul says.

'Yes. But you aren't making breakfast today.
I am.
Just go.
Won't you be late?'

'I make Ready Brek when you've
already left for work, Ana. Every day.'

And here it comes,
the litany of my failures,
the list of times I am absent,
the reminder of all the hours Paul has committed to this
and I have not.
                    My failed wifehood.

'Make it for him now then if you're so perfect.'

Paul rolls his eyes,
goes to the bottom of the stairs
and struggles into a pair of polished brogues.
        The smartness does not suit him.
He comes back to kiss the kids.
Murmurs to me,
'What's going on, Ana?'

He is serious.
It is a question he wants answered,
not the start of an argument.

'The truth?'

'Yes.'

'I'm tired, Paul. That's the truth.
I'm so fucking tired.'

∾

I drop off the kids, sign them up for late club
and take a train to Liverpool.
Towns blur by –
        Stafford, Crewe, Runcorn.
And shops –
        Sainsbury's, Next, Pets at Home.
Then
        houses with windows missing, frames covered in black bin bags.

I am inside time.
I am nowhere in space.
I buy a KitKat from the food trolley.

At Liverpool Lime Street station I use the toilet,
buy a packet of nuts
and head home.

Paul says, as I remove my scarf,
'I got the job. I'll be the new deputy in January.'

He is perfect for the position,
willing to shout on some days,
but mostly reasonable.

'Well done,' I say.
Ruth and Jon are watching cartoons.

I should have gone to Glasgow.

ॐ

I went Interrailing when I was nineteen.
Tanya didn't get any further than Calais,
meeting a man on the ferry-crossing
and deciding he was a better summer bet than I was.
            Of course.

I wore Birkenstocks every day that summer.
            Of course.
Ate fresh fried doughnuts.
Tried to mobilise an interest in cathedrals and fountains.

On the way home I sat with a woman from Denmark.
She was Viking, bewitching.
'You look healthy but not happy to have travelled,' she said.
'Maybe it's good you go home now.
Or maybe home is the problem.'

The way she contemplated me
        as I picked anything green from my salad
was unsettling.

'I've been a bit lonely on the trip,' I told her.
This despite having slept with a hot
Hungarian the previous day.

'I don't know,' she said.
She folded her hands in her lap.
Her hair was grey but she wasn't old.
She wore oversized hoopy earrings.
'Loneliness is something we are taught, I think.'

I shrugged. I wasn't much for self-analysis.
I had taken many photos to prove I had been somewhere.
I'd bought souvenirs for Nora and Mum.
I'd pierced my bellybutton in Barcelona.

'Sometimes children must embrace this lonely feeling.
To survive. You understand?
You reach for loneliness maybe and maybe it is a gift.
To be lonely and to be OK.'

I opened a book to stop her talking.
Eventually she fell asleep and I moved seats.

Because she was right.
Also, I didn't want to have to say goodbye.

∾

Ruth is dancing around the dining table.
Jon is following, butting her like a goat,
        holding tight to the belt of her dressing gown.
She is singing.
Jon is trying to copy her
but he doesn't know all the words.
        'Here is the beehive,
        Where are the bees?
        Hidden away where nobody sees.
        Watch and you'll see them
                come out of the hive.
        One, two, three, four, five!'
Ruth sniffs a vase of wilting tulips.
        'Buzz, buzz, buzz, buzz, buzz.'

'Everyone bathed and ready for bed?' I ask.

The kids continue skipping.
        'Here is the beehive,
        Where are the bees?
        Hidden away where nobody sees.

Watch and you'll see them
        land on the floor.
One, two, three, four!
Buzz, buzz, buzz, buzz.'

'Where's Daddy?' I ask.

They wave but otherwise ignore me.
The song goes on.
        'Here is the beehive,
        Where are the bees?
        Hidden away where nobody sees.
        Watch and you'll see them
                come out of the tree.
        One, two, three!
        Buzz, buzz, buzz.'

'Stop it!' I shout.
'You're making me dizzy.'

The song skids to a halt.
'Sorry, Mummy,' Ruth says,
        running to me,
                wrapping her arms around my legs.

'At the end, all the bees fly away,' Jon tells me.
'Don't they, Ruthie?'

My daughter lets go of my legs.
'Yes, that's how it ends,' she says.
'Buzzzz … they've all flown away.'

ঌ

I leave the office at lunchtime
with a rucksack,
                    no laptop or papers,
and walk up the High Road.
My cuticles are dry, cracked.
I haven't bothered with a manicure in weeks.
I walk right by Crystal Nail Designs
        to the yoga place,
                frosted glass on the front,
                everything clean.
                        White.

Inside the studio
women wait, relaxed into child's pose,
water bottles and blocks beside them.
The soles of their feet are smooth.

Three minutes until the class begins.
I have eaten nothing.
My stomach whines.

And then she arrives, smiles at familiar faces
and finds a spot at the front.
In the mirror she sees me,
        turns,
            waves in an exaggerated way.
I try to look dizzy,
surprised to see her.
I am not, of course.
I am here because she is here,
because we arranged our meetings around Rebecca's hobbies,
and I was certain I would see her.
'Hey!' I whisper. 'Speak to you after?'

'Definitely.'
She finds child's pose, cat cow, down dog, plank.

ॐ

You said Rebecca could drink two bottles of wine
and chase them down with gin
on a weeknight.
I pretended to be concerned.

Really I wanted to hear how unsettled she was –
        how utterly repellent.

ॐ

'Shall we go for a sneaky cocktail?' I ask Rebecca.

She looks at her Apple Watch.
'It's still a bit early for me,' she says.

We sit opposite one another
in Dan & DeCarlo,
smiling awkwardly
as the barista clears away dirty mugs, stained napkins.
'I've never seen you at a class before,' Rebecca says.

'I normally go after work.'

'Ah, that explains it.'
Next to us, three teenagers
slouch against one another,
sharing a drink from a takeaway cup.

'How are you?' I ask.

'Oh, you know. Good days and bad days.
Everything ticking along your end?'

'Yes,' I say. One of the teenagers is watching me,
        a girl with raw acne across her cheeks and forehead.
'I needed that class today though.'

Rebecca raises her eyebrows.
'Is work stressful? I don't know how you do it.
I haven't the stomach for office work.'

The girl is fingering her spotty face.
'Oh no. *Life* is stressful. Families. Children. Men.'

'Yeah. You don't miss them until you need them.
You know what I miss? Being spontaneous.
A friend offered me a ticket for the ballet last week
but I hadn't anyone to watch the boys.
I'm trapped. It sounds selfish but ... '

'No. I understand.'

A pause.

'And if that happens again, call me.
I'm not far. I can come over and babysit.'

She laughs. 'That's way beyond the call of duty.'

'I mean it,' I say, and I do.
'A night away from my husband would be bliss.
            Sorry, that was insensitive.'

Rebecca pulls her chair closer.

It scrapes loudly against the floor.
She is plastered in make-up, false eyelashes.
Her nails are painted with a coral-coloured gel.
'Not at all. Life's hard. Everyone has something.'

'Yeah,' I say, as though I find her very knowing.
'I suppose no one's marriage is perfect.
And it's only when the worst happens
you appreciate what you did have.'
I watch her for tics, tells.

The teenagers scream and fall into one another.
I remember that sort of love.
          For friends.
I thought it would always mean more than anything else.

Rebecca searches in her handbag
and pulls out a breakfast bar.
She opens it and offers to share.
I shake my head.
'Connor and I weren't doing great at the end,' she says.
          Something leaps in me,
                              dances.
          A rush of breath explodes in my chest.
'We were a Mr and Mrs to the world.'
The girls squeal again and Rebecca hesitates.
'It doesn't matter now, I suppose.
As you say, it's probably normal.

We were married a long time.
Three kids.
Life.'

'Did you love him?'
The words are between us before I can stop myself.

'What sort of question is that?' Rebecca is serious.

'I only meant ... '

She looks at the wall clock. 'No. I'm too tetchy.
Sleep is a city I rarely visit, I'm afraid.'

When we leave, we head in opposite directions.
I stop off at Crystal Nail Designs
before going back to work.
I get gel nails.
A very classy coral colour.

∾

Ruth loses a tooth,
          stands on the toilet seat to appraise
          the grisliness of her blood-filled mouth
          in the bathroom mirror.
We wrap her baby tooth in tissue, hide it beneath the pillow
for the fairy to find

and conjure into cash.
'Clean ones make the most. Lucky you're a good brusher,' I say,
turning out the light.

'Magic isn't real,' she mutters. 'I know that.'

'Of course it is,' I say.

She pulls the duvet over her head.
'It isn't. You're being a liar.'

Children know everything.
Even the things we think they do not know,
       they sense in their stomachs.

What am I doing to my children?

                ᕣ

It is below zero.
Parisians walk
with their chins uncharacteristically tucked
       into their chests.
Isolated snowflakes flurry in the hard wind.

I hadn't thought to pack a hat,
couldn't admit to winter
in November,
         the death months.

I buy a cheap nylon one
from a luggage shop on rue Vieille du Temple,
take a photo to text home,
            red-nosed, hair concealed.
I remembered to bring Rebecca's gloves though,
the blue striking against my black coat.
On the train Tanya said, 'Not your usual thing.'
She fondled them, sniffed the leather.

This is her birthday treat to me:
            the Eurostar,
            shopping,
            steak-frites.
But she is ill with flu, won't leave the room,
begged the concierge to send up
a kettle, mug, tea bags – which he did –
though the tea was Lipton, so now
she is making me search the streets
for anything 'with a bit more kick'.

In a café across the street from the hotel
I scroll through Rebecca's Instagram.
She has not posted anything since you died –
            I suppose it would be in bad taste –
so I examine her old photos:
overpriced fabric samples,
rugby matches,
sunsets.

The waiter is wary.
I have nursed a hot chocolate for two hours.
'*L'addition*,' I say.
I will not tip him.
In Paris it is not a requirement.
The French are devoutly unambiguous.

I buy some Barry's tea
and present my find to Tanya,
along with a newspaper she can't read,
stolen from reception.

'Did you book dinner?'

'Philosophe,' I say. Tanya nods,
clicking the kettle
as I slip into the en suite.

The shower has mould in the grout.
The water is lukewarm.
The hairdryer cracks up mid dry
and I try not to cry,
even though everything is difficult and broken.

Tanya is back in bed.
'Shall we get a train home tonight?'

'Please,' I say.

St Pancras is warmer than Paris.
I shop in the parade,
have a glass of beer in Granary Square.
I cannot go home.

The thought of it.

I find a Premier Inn behind the station.
I like the purple and yellow colour scheme,
the soap attached to the wall,
the working hairdryer
and the non-existent receptionists.

I will sleep until housekeeping wake me.

&

When we shared hotel rooms overnight,
I used the toilets in restaurants, lobbies, shops,
so you wouldn't have to know anything about my shit.

And you did the same for me, I believe.

The fucking romance.

&

I have watched, over and over,
clips of Marina Abramović meeting Ulay
to say goodbye somewhere near the middle
of the Great Wall of China:
> *The Lovers*, 1988.
They smile for pictures, embrace for the last time.
> How did they stick to this plan?
> We will meet, and we will part
>> forever.
Paul catches me crying as I replay another moment,
twenty-two years later in the lives of the two,
> face to face again
> at the MOMA,
Marina arresting in red,
> Ulay adjusting his trouser legs as he sits,
both confronted by something
they once loved.

Paul says, 'You're so sappy.'

They have their love, their art.
> They respected this with ceremony.
How could I not cry?

> ❧

I never got the chance to say goodbye.

> ❧

Paul is shouting.
'You can swan off to Paris for three days
but your kids get sick and work suddenly matters again.'

'I *booked* that time off. And it was *two* days.
I didn't book anything off this week.
I've clients back to back.'

'And I have classes, plus a parents' evening.
I suppose that stuff doesn't matter.
I'm just a teacher.
"Those who can't—"'

'Stop screaming. Ruth's awake.'
I seize his sleeve but he brushes me off.
'You can't just let me do something nice
without punishing me for it, can you?'

Paul throws a stack of exercise books into a plastic box.
'I'm going.'

I want to say, *I can't. Don't leave me. How do I do this?*

He says, 'Don't forget to feed them,'
and slams the front door.

Ruth is perched at the top of the stairs.
She is naked but for one sock.
'I have a scratchy neck,' she says.

'Come down to me, sweetness.'
I kiss her toes,
give her a dose of Calpol and tuck her up on the sofa
with endless episodes of *My Little Pony*.

'You were shouting,' she says.

'Daddy was shouting,' I correct her.

In the kitchen I swallow down some painkillers
with a slug of Calpol.

'Jesus, Ana.
I don't think I can do this any more.'
It is Paul.
Back again.
Watching.
Changing his jacket.
           And he leaves.

Upstairs, Jon cries, 'Daddy? Daddy? Mum?'

Ruth runs upstairs to comfort her brother.

I can't do this any more
either.

❧

Paul asked me to marry him in a Pizza Hut on the A10.
We'd missed the start of *Winter's Bone*
because *I'd* missed the earlier bus,
so in a huff he'd refused to go into the cinema.

We'd just moved in together,
spent most of our weekends in IKEA's marketplace
and painting the flat in bright colours
only ever befitting a rental.

I got a deep pan Hawaiian and a salad bowl
piled high with cucumber and croutons,
wondered what my friends were up to.

'I love you,' he said. 'You're always late, but I love you.'
'I love you,' I told him. 'You're a control freak, but I love you.'
We refilled our glasses with Diet Coke.

In the car park a woman in a BMW couldn't
reverse her car into a space
wide enough to park a mobile home.
'That'll be you in a few years,' he said.
'Piss off,' I replied.
'I love her baseball cap,' he said. 'And I like rich women!'

We still talked about money like it was a fantasy
that belonged to the future,
to other people,

to adults –
which we weren't quite prepared to admit
we'd become.

'Will you marry me?' Paul said.
I was keeping tabs on the ice cream factory in the corner:
tubs of Smarties and dolly mixtures,
strawberry and chocolate sauces in giant sticky bottles.

'Are you joking?'

'Not really. As I explained, I love you.'

He reached into the pocket of his messenger bag
and pulled out a burgundy box.
                                        'Here.'

Inside was a gold ring.
No diamond, an amethyst at its centre.
'I can get you something else.
Something garish if you like –
            to go with a BMW.'

I used a napkin to wipe away tears.
Then I slipped the ring on to my finger.
'It's really me,' I said. 'Thank you.'

'Sorry about the film.
I know you wanted to see it.'

'Sorry I was late. We can rent it.'

'So shall we do it then? At some point.
Get married, I mean.
Happy to see the film too though.'
Paul was looking sheepishly into his untouched pizza.

'OK,' I said. 'I'd really like that.'

It was a garish, traditional wedding.

∾

Paul and I speak in grunts and nods.
The children look first to me, then him,
           trying to interpret our maze of silence.
We are all sick now.
Everyone stuck at home
coughing, shivering, not showering.

I make the children fresh honey, lemon and ginger tea,
and back in bed we watch *The Goonies*.
           'You'll love it!' I tell them.
           Because I love it.
But *The Goonies* is too scary.
Sloth is strange.
There is a dead man in the freezer.
I had forgotten about all the kissing.

When Paul trudges downstairs drenched in self-pity,
Ruth and Jon
jump up,
squeeze him as though he has returned from the wilds;
they are glad to see him alive.
'Mum gave us jelly,' Jon says.
His tongue is green. He is still in his pyjamas.

'To cool our throats,' Ruth says,
sensing Paul may not approve of my mothering.

He is not listening.
He is heading for the front door.
'Didn't you hear the banging?' he complains,
opening it. In walks his mother, Leanna Williams,
ablaze in a suit the colour of sweetcorn.
'I'm sorry I couldn't come earlier, my darling.
I had a hair appointment.
Oh, hello, Ana.
I thought you'd be at work.'

'I thought she would too,' Paul says.

Ruth skips around the coffee table.
Jon has given himself a paper cut, cries.
'We're on the mend. You didn't need to come,' I say.
    And I wish you hadn't, you old bitch.

'I brought Berocca,' she says.
'And smoked salmon. Who's hungry?'

Paul kisses her powdery cheek.
'Thanks for coming, Mum,' he said. 'We'd be lost.'

Leanna settles herself on the sofa. The kids join her.

'Tea?' Paul asks.

I follow him into the kitchen.
The butter is open on the countertop.
Paul uses his forearm to push it aside.
'Shouldn't she be making *you* the tea?
Has she come for a holiday?'

Paul fills the kettle using bottled water.
Not looking up, he says,
'Have you thought about moving out?
Maybe you should start looking for places.'

'Me? I'm not leaving the kids.'

He clicks the kettle. It growls gently.
'Well. Someone should go.'

In the doorway, Ruth is watching us.

PART FOUR

The agent, a girl no older than twenty,
pushes open the door
and curls a nostril.
'They must have pets,' she says.

The mat is littered in mail, more discarded behind the door,
along with a broken umbrella,
a tool box.

And two grey cats do appear,
                                        bony and matted.
'So it's twenty-two hundred per month.
Three bed.
One bath.
Sixth-month minimum lease.'
The agent leads me into the kitchen.
Saucepans are piled high in the sink.
The surface of the dining table is invisible beneath a mess
of oil paints and monochrome canvases.
'Not bad really for the price.
This area can get silly.'

'I live close by,' I explain,
wondering why I'm trying to impress this child.

'Are you renovating?'

'No, I'm separating.
I'm looking for a place for myself and my new partner.
He has three boys.
I have a girl and boy.'

'Right.'
She is distracted by the smell, isn't attending to my lies.

But I continue, as she leads me upstairs
into bedrooms with bed sheets for curtains.
'I guess we're a typical blended family.
His ex isn't completely on board, but these things take time.
Main focus is the kids now.
And retaining my dignity.'

'Uh huh. So I'm showing someone else the house later.
If you're interested you'll need financial references
and to let me know as soon as.'

The plughole in the shower is caked in hair.
Bile rises in my throat.
'It's a shithole,' I say.
'I'm not interested. But call me if anything better
becomes available.'

Ruth and Jon will be asleep already.
Paul will be scrubbing pans.
And I am here trying to torpedo them all.
This family I have made.

It is almost dark outside.
My phone rings. It is Rebecca.
'Hi, Ana! How are you?'

'I'm well. You?'

'OK, I know this is going to sound cheeky
but you said I could call if I needed someone
to watch the boys.'

'What time shall I come over?'

∾

The trampoline was speckled with conifer detritus.
They spiked the soles of my feet.
Patches of the mat were damp.
You didn't care:
bounced on your knees,
spun in the air,
star-jumped,
until the motion made me nauseous.
'Come on,' you said. 'Jump with me,' you said.

It was our first time together in a house,
a detached cottage rental in Gloucester,
better-suited to a family than the two of us.

What could we possibly do with all that space
when we were used to narrow hotel rooms,
maids knocking at nine.

'We should have brought the kids,' you said.

'And our spouses.' It was a joke
I was fond of making,
suggesting we look for ways to bring
Rebecca and Paul together –
        'If only they'd meet someone,' you said.
        If only they'd die, I thought.

Inside, after pasta and sex,
we lay on the couch listening to Smooth FM,
not talking until I said,
'Have you ever thought about hiding your assets?'

'Is it possible to hide anything these days?'

'You hide me.'

We were silent until you asked if I'd be willing to live in Iceland.
I said I would, so we shook on it,
agreed Iceland in the summer,
Lisbon in the winter.
And we went to bed.

The next day in town we chose a sofa.
I wanted the brown velvet, you preferred blue,
but we settled,
        at least, on a button-back style,
and pretended to watch TV on it,
though we were staring out the first-floor window
at vans
passing by in the downpour.
            'We cooperate so well.
            We should live together,' you said.

'Paul and I are splitting up,' I told you.
'He doesn't want to but I want you. It's decided.
Are you leaving Rebecca, or is this it?'

'You aren't splitting up.' You seemed scared.

'I'm leaving him.'

'Oh, come on, Ana.
All I do is hurt you, Ana.
You realise that, don't you?'

Back at the house we sat inside, stared out at the trampoline.
            It wasn't easy to remember what I had felt the previous day.
            The freedom of jumping.
            The sting of it.

You topped up my glass with rosé.
'It's *you* I love,' you said,
inching your chair away from mine to catch some sun.

It went that way.
> When I wanted more,
> you punished me with distance.

∾

Paul cried.

I hadn't seen him do that much,
> even when his brother died.

'You'll destroy our family,' he said,
and, 'I don't understand,'
and, 'The kids are tiny. They're tiny.'
He curled into a ball in the bed,
wouldn't let me touch him,
eventually refused to listen.

I'm not sure he slept.
Ruth had a party the next day at Belmont Farm.
We went as a family,
fed goats from the flats of our hands.

You messaged a photo of David in his cricket kit
as I queued for cake.
　　　　My husband couldn't speak.
　　　　He was crushed.
　　　　And I had caused it.
　　　　We had.

While your life ticked by unaltered.

And Rebecca?

　　　　Oblivious.
　　　　Happy and stupid.

❧

In the kitchen, your sons are perched around the table like statues.
Rebecca presses her hand into the top of each head.
'This is Ned, David and Jamie.
These two guys staying here have promised to leave you alone.
Haven't you? Did you choose a film?'

Only the youngest nods.
'We're gonna watch something with boobs.'

'Jamie!' Rebecca laughs. I am supposed to do the same.
'*You're* going to go to bed in a half hour. Right?'

Your eldest reaches for another slice of garlic bread.
His head is shaved.
He has a tiny monogram tattoo on his thumb: CM.
Your middle child, David, scans me like he knows everything.
        'Who are you?' He has your teeth. Nose.
He is wearing lots of braided bracelets.

Each of your boys is painted in a little bit of you.

'I'm Ana,' I say.

'Mum's friend?' David eats with his mouth open.
You did that sometimes. It wasn't a thing I disliked.

'I hope your husband doesn't mind us borrowing you?' Rebecca says.

Around the kitchen, stocky candles have been lit.
'Oh, he doesn't mind. Time alone with the TV suits him!'

I messaged Paul to say I had a client meeting.
He didn't respond:
                he has given up trying to understand.

'We won't be too long.'
Ned stands
and with a grunt follows Rebecca into the hallway.

'David will show you where the coffee's kept.
Thank you for doing this.
        You're so good.'

❧

I get into Jamie's bed and read to him,
laughing, laughing,
as we turn the pages,
as Mr Gum and Billy William
drink beer and belch.
                'You're so sweet,' I say,
and your youngest rests his head against my chest.

❧

        'Stay for a Prosecco,'
Rebecca pleads, arriving home and
rattling on about how well
Ned is performing at school.
        'OK,' I say.
        I say, 'OK,'
and we drink until midnight.

Look at me now, Connor Mooney.

Just look.

❧

When I think of the things
I almost said,
            the flotsam
                        in my head,
a hand tightens around my throat.

I wish I could speak simply
or simply speak,
whisper the wrecking yard junk
hidden in my pokiest corners.

But there is little meaning in the slant of words
unless a listener replies.

And your reply is forever silence.

❧

After the firm's Christmas do,
            a curry on East End Road with thick red wine,
Tanya and I take a cab to a seedy nightclub in Holloway.
'I should go home,' I say, but don't.

I do shots at the bar,
dance in my coat
with my bag on my shoulder.

In the toilets
two girls in leather skirts
stop kissing to say,
          'You're lush for someone your age,'
and press a pill
between my lips.
          The brunette leans forward, licks my mouth.
          'Well lush,' she says, peering into me
          until the other girl pulls her back,
          devours her hungrily.

I dance again,
drink,
barrel against clubbers until the bouncer throws me
          out.

I wait for Tanya across the road in a kebab shop.

I am mumbling to myself, but I don't know how to stop.
'It's the pill. It's the pill,' I am saying.

The chef laughs.
I threaten to fight him.
He laughs again and so does a hipster.
'You only get away with that sort of shit when you're eighteen,'
the hipster says. 'Bit sad when you're fifty.'

'Fifty?' I push him.
He staggers gently,
bites into his burger.
Ketchup from the side drips on to the floor,
        too gloopy to be blood.

They laugh harder than before.
I am funny. But I do not want to be funny.

        I want to fight.
        I want to lose.

                    ∽

Snow has settled overnight
        though the forecast promised rain.

Tree branches crack, drop lumps of ice.
The postman hasn't yet been.

I poach eggs, the yolks bright as small clementines.
Outside, Ruth and Jon are giggling, arguing.

Paul shovels snow,
        glares in at me now and then,
        perhaps because I am in my dressing gown,
        perhaps because he heard me throwing up when I got home.

Ruth is building a snow-throne using her bare hands.
Jon is whining about a ruined snow angel,
        his pinching wellies.

He shouts, 'Come outside, Mummy!'
Ruth raps on the window. 'It's quite OK. Isn't it, Daddy?'

'Breakfast in two minutes.'

The eggs are rubbery.
The toast popped too long ago to be butterable.

Paul tosses aside his shovel, comes indoors.
'Your shift,' he says. 'I'm going back to bed.
By the way, Ruth has swimming at ten.
Jon has a party at twelve.
I already texted you the details.
I'm busy all day.'

'What are you doing?'

He laughs and, leaving the room, says,
'I know that isn't a real question.'

ॐ

We met in Cherry Tree Wood,
sat on a bench and watched parents whittle away their time,
pushing swings.
'I just think we should sort out our marriages
then find one another afterwards,' you said.

'How long will it take?' I asked.

'I don't know,' you said.

I wanted to be reasonable,
to say I understood
and yes
and of course
and anything you need.

I said, 'So you and Rebecca go to therapy
and I just wait for it to be over
with no knowledge of which way it'll go?'
I was eating a sandwich for lunch,
rewrapped it in its paper.

A mother pushed with one hand,
checked her phone with the other.
By her feet were three bags of groceries,
one toppled, onions spilling out on to the rubber mulch.

'I love you,' you said,
and I wanted to hold on to that,
but what part of loving me meant giving me up?
                                                    Again.

'She deserves closure.
Counselling would give her that.
I can't just walk out.
People don't just walk out, Ana.'
'Ask me to walk out and I'll do it,' I said.
'I want this. I don't just *say* I want this.'

A small girl tried to straddle the swaying seat of the zip line.
'You can do it, darling,' her mother said encouragingly.
But she did not go forward to help.
At her ankles a toy poodle yelped.

'You know how hard this is.
Stop pretending it isn't hard.
And stop pretending you're free and single.
You're trapped too.
You make out this mess is my doing.'

'The indecision is your doing,' I said.

You stood. Your shoes were dusty.
The sun was on your face, but I didn't find you handsome –
        I thought you looked pathetic,
        like so many of the men

I saw traipsing through the office to meet with Tanya:

Help me help me I've fucked up my life
Help me help me to win back my wife.

'I have to go to back to work. If you want to talk, call me later.'

'But not at the weekend and not after five.'
My voice was as light as the afternoon birdsong.
It was the way to anger you
    and anger was better than indifference.

'Stop trying to bully me,' you said, and walked away.

The small girl had abandoned the zip line.
She climbed the stairs to the slide.
Some things are unconquerable alone.

❧

Rebecca Didn't Love You.
                She told you so.
            And you believed her.
She said, 'I don't love you either, Connor.'

But
you believed your mother, who said,
Marriage is work. That's the point.
It isn't meant to be easy.
And

you polled your friends,
who all had different opinions:
If you aren't in love, leave.
Sex isn't the be-all and end-all of things.

So you stayed,
returned from days of passion
to nights of silence
and convinced yourself it was
normal
and enough
and at the very least
what you deserved.
But did you ever ask yourself
what I deserved?

ော

'It's chocolates,' I say.
            The caretaker
                        shakes his head.
'Can't you take them as a holiday gift?'

The snow has turned to slush.
The car park is empty.
The children are already in assembly
and I am running late for work.

A silver Nissan is stuck in the school driveway,
    all available men
    helping haul it over stubborn ice
    along with Miss Roach the nursery teacher.

'Are you Muslim?' I ask.

'I'm Jehovah's Witness,' he says.
'I'm not offended, but I can't take it.'
I'm surprised he doesn't mutter this.

'What about New Year?
    Do you celebrate that?'

Another mother steps in beside us –
Lycra leggings, body warmer, bright new trainers.
'Can we get your help, Sammy?'
    She points to the car,
    the men straining against its metal body.
She doesn't say,
    I'm already late for yin yoga, hun.

'It's just sweets,' I continue.
'Can't your kids eat a few sweets?'

The head teacher smiled at her bottle of wine,
the class teacher did the same,
chocolates for everyone else –
      office staff, kitchen,
        Mr Syed the caretaker.

I didn't forget you! I want to yell.
None of these parents give a shit
      but I got you truffles.

'It's a kind gesture.' He moves away.

The yoga-mum pokes his arm,
      says something and he laughs.

The present is still in my hands.

～

Nora and Phil are wearing matching jumpers and
keep touching – hands reaching, eyes dancing.
'You shouldn't get pissed if you're pregnant,' I say.

'I think three kids is enough, don't you?' she says.
'I know this is going to sound tragic, but he's being so nice.
I can't help liking him when he's, well, not a cunt.
He made dinner last night.
And he's booked for me to have a massage on Thursday.'

'Is he seeing escorts?'

Nora reaches for a handful of Quality Street.
'Why are you the way you are?' She is not annoyed.

The turkey is resting. I take out the potatoes.
Paul and Phil have gone to the park with the kids.
The dinner will be cold if they don't get home soon.

'But I mean, genuinely, what's with you lately?
You're too distracted to even put me down properly.'

'Have you any more Valium?'

'Tell me.'

'Paul and I are splitting up.'

Nora hands me a hard caramel.
'That isn't it,' she says. 'That isn't what I mean.
Are you cheating on him?
Are you having an affair?'

❦

It is in the pause
following a simple question
where the liar is uncovered.

∾

We met to exchange gifts.

In Cherry Tree Wood again,
a place we knew wouldn't end with us in bed.

It had been three weeks since our last contact.
Your jumper was thick with cat hair.
You were carrying a duffle bag.
       I didn't feel I could ask where you'd been,
             where you were going.

You weighed my present on your knees.
'Can I unwrap it later?'

'Sure.'
But I did open the gift you'd given me.
A bracelet. Gold with one enamel heart charm attached
            like an afterthought.
I didn't know what it meant.
And I wanted it to have meaning.

'How's the counselling going?' I asked.

You shrugged. 'Hard. She cries through most sessions.
I've taken on the role of Chief Bastard.
She can't understand what's happened.'

'Wouldn't it be kinder to just tell her?'
'Ana.'
'Did the counsellor give you homework?
Have you been told to go on some dates?
Have more sex?'

'Ana.'

'Are you staying with her?' I asked desperately.
'Do you still love her?'

You opened your mouth to answer but
nothing
came out.

❧

Nora and Phil have done their January sale shopping
        online.
        It is not even nine o'clock.
Paul is humming, keeps asking who's up for Monopoly.
He has had too much beer.
The five cousins are piled together on the sofa,
trying not to sleep. The bickering has simmered.

In the loo I check Rebecca's Instagram.
She is not at home.
She is somewhere sunny,
            has taken a picture of her toes in the sand,
            a Christmassy cocktail in hand.
She is trumpeting her joy.

'I'm popping out for a bit,' I call out.

Nora rushes into the hall.
'Where the fuck are you going? It's Christmas Day.'

'I'm taking Tanya her present.
I haven't been drinking. Check my breath.'
I exhale into her face.
                        She shoves me.
'I've made up the beds if you're tired,' I say.

Christmas is over and
I am no longer responsible for anyone's seasonal good cheer.
I have made mince pies and
the stuffing was my best yet:
            fresh cranberries and hazelnuts.
The children still believe in Santa Claus.

Driving away in Paul's car, I call Tanya.
'If anyone asks, I'm at your house.'

In the background, slurred singing.
'Roger that. Hope you're up to no good.
God, you are always so *good*.
I bought you perfume but I opened it.
Smells gorgeous on me.
Happy Christmas, my sweet.'

I drive up and down Devon Rise,
past your house several times before parking.

Your driveway is empty.
In your neighbour's window,
a cat is sleeping next to an electric menorah.
      A streetlight flickers, hasn't the will to remain.
All else is darkness.

I cut the engine, watch for movement, step out of the car.
I am still wearing a paper hat.
If you were to appear in your office window and see me now,
      what would you say?
      But seriously,
      what would you say?

Your gate groans.
The neighbour's cat raises its head, its tail.
I slip the card for Rebecca through the cold brass letterbox.
      Don't worry, it isn't the sort I threatened to write,
      to expose you. Unleash chaos.

It is an ordinary Christmas card,
The Madonna Suckling the Christ Child, Carlo Dolci,
the message cool and kind.

I trace the glass panel in the front door.
Did you ever touch that part?
Where do your fingerprints persist?
On the painted grey woodwork?

The side gate next to the garage is open.
Instead of closing it, I go through.
Fog loiters above wet ground.

I rest on a rattan seat and light a cigarette.
The lawn is untidy.
Your sons' football goals have collapsed into the grass.
A broom is prostrate on the patio.

A fox cuts across the garden,
spotting me, stopping,
staring into the night, at the indecisive glint
at the end of my cigarette.

Paul texts.
Enough is enough, Ana.

And he is right.
Enough is enough.

∽

The only time you ever visited my home
you treated it like it was your own:
          boots off at the door,
grubbing in cupboards for a cafetière.

I couldn't sit comfortably on the sofa
in case someone saw us through the window.
I wouldn't open the back door
in case we were heard
by the neighbours.

I pretended to be ashamed of the mess –
          'Try not to look,' I said;
I'd spent a full week
clearing out, cleaning up, erasing evidence of my living.
Even the wheelie bins got a bleachy rinse out.
I wanted my domesticity to seduce you,
but hadn't counted on you being hungry,
wanting something hot.

I sliced a farmhouse loaf for toast,
made loose-leaf Earl Grey,
which you found hilarious.

You reminded me of my meagre offering
often –
letting me know
I wasn't as perfect as I pretended.

Thing is, that day I found out you like
pale toast with margarine.
What the fuck does that say about a person?

～

Mum spent Christmas in Bruges,
so it's lunch in Crouch End for New Year's Day.
'It's so noisy,' Paul complains. 'And pricey.
Couldn't we have eaten at home?'

Ruth and Jon flank my mother,
holding out their chocolatey hands as she pulls surprises
from a carrier bag,
none of them wrapped:
football stickers for an album no one owns,
liquorice and Bic biros,
Uno.

Nora catches my eye.
It was the same when we were kids.
A Mr Kipling birthday cake and a kiss.
'I love you, my feather,' she'd say.
Mum stares at the iPad we got her
as though I've bought her a can of tuna,
then sets it aside, unopened,
to concentrate on her raspberry torte.
'I'll have it if she doesn't want it,' Ruth says.
'I bloody will,' Paul says.

Phil is flirting with a woman by the bar,
     a blonde.
     Nora pretends not to see.
The kids pound on a fruit machine.

It is time to go.

I order another bottle of wine for the table.
Mum moves her chair close.
'If only he'd be more blatant with his cheating,' she whispers.
'Then Nora could leave. No blame.
I felt the same way for years about your dad.
Finally he put me out of my misery.'

'You're drunk,' I say.
'He cheated a hundred times and you allowed it.'

'You're always so sad, Ana,' she replies.
'What you don't realise is that nobody wants that for you.
And you shouldn't want it for yourself.'

∽

We had fallen back into togetherness
and I knew every argument you were having with Rebecca,
every unkind thing she'd said.

I was back to knowing your movements –
      the day you were at the dentist,
      the times you had to collect the kids,
      the mornings you had meetings.

It was a Thursday.

You had a couples counselling appointment for eleven
so I fasted until twelve thirty,
      until I was sure it was over,
knew no one was encouraging closeness,
reminding you how to connect,
asking you to pause to see one another
               and forcing
                  me   out.

How did you meet?
How did you fall in love?
Tell me about those first days.

I imagined the room's wide windows,
Somewhere looking on to a lake.
Ferns outside – wet with raindrops.

Whatever it was
it was not a box of lies,
like our hotel rooms,
small and smelling of other people's mornings.

I imagined Rebecca's tears without sympathy,
hoping you'd see through her
and finally
say,
    'It's someone else I love.'

At two o'clock you messaged.
I'd eaten a grapefruit by then,
written up a couple of wills.

Hope you're keeping well today,
        was all you wrote.

Hope you're keeping well.

∾

Mum reads *The Cat in the Hat* aloud to the children. Drinks gin.

Watching her, Nora says, 'She fell over in Belgium, you know.
Claimed a bat attacked her. She was pissed.'

'Naturally.'

Nora tuts.
'Right, you lot, we have a tree and a whole heap of
Christmas spirit to take down tomorrow.

I'm not waiting until the sixth. Christmas is done.
Come on, let's go.'

Paul chases Ruth and Jon upstairs, runs the bath.
Mum waves to Nora from the window
        as my sister's car pulls away.
'I'm dating,' Mum says,
collapsing again into the sofa.
'He's Dutch, but he lives in Islamabad.'

'What are you talking about, Mum?'

'My boyfriend. He grew up in Amsterdam.
He's an American Navy Seal now.
Do you have any Jaffa cakes?'

'Ana!' Paul calls out. The bath is run.
It is my turn to attend to the children.

'Where did you meet him?' I ask.

'I haven't yet. He's coming to visit in the spring.
He's gorgeous. Much younger than I am.'

'From Islamabad?'

'Yes, Ana, from Islamabad.'

'So basically you're dating an online scammer.

How much money has he asked for?'

She sits up.
'What did you just say to me?'

'Holy Christ, Mum. How much have you given him?'

'You know what?
I'm lonely and you and Nora don't seem to care. He does.
He messages every morning and every night.
He wants to know how I am and where I am.'
        I shake my head.
'I'm not allowed to be in love.
Is that what you're saying, Ana?'

'He doesn't even exist!' I shout.

Paul is in the doorway.
'Who doesn't exist?' he wants to know.

∾

We were two weeks late for Hogmanay
but took a celebratory trip to Edinburgh nonetheless.
        Our three-year anniversary.
        Three years.

While you slept,
panic filled my throat.
I furled myself into a juddering ball

at the edge of the bed
until the shaking got so bad I woke you,
        begged you to take me to the hospital
        because I was dying.
                'I'm sure it's a stroke,' I said.
        I couldn't see, had no feeling in my hands.

I was thinking of Jon.
How likely it was I wouldn't even be a memory to him
if I died that night.

You'd have been fine without me.

        You pulled me into you,
        used your arms to press out the pain,
        assured me nothing fatal was happening.
        'This isn't forever, Ana,' you told me.

And that was the crux of it.
We were never forever.
Always in a place of
                passing.
Everything that mattered happened in locked rooms.
Nothing came out of them.

        You didn't call an ambulance but
        got up and arranged for an early
        flight to take us home.

Leaving, I said, 'I survived the night.'
You hitched up your jeans,
tightened your belt and I regretted
    not asking you to hit me with it,
    so I could feel the buckle against my back.
    Again the word *beautiful* came to mind.
    The room was drowning in amber light.
    Your face in it against the dawn.
    Beautiful.

You left the housekeeper a tip.
'Yup. You're alive. It's amazing.'

Why wouldn't you ever believe me
when I told you I was dying?

                        ℘

No matter how carefully
I put it away,
I can never find the fairy
for the top of the
Christmas tree
until it is January,
and too late,
the tree rusting in a skip somewhere.

PART FIVE

First day back, Rebecca calls the office.
My stomach dips, dives, just as it did when you'd call.
'Thanks for the card,' she says.
'It was so thoughtful of you.
You've been a rock. Really.'

'How are you?'

'We were away but back now in the scrum of it.
Washing and dinner and the usual.
I was wondering when probate is likely to wrap up.'

Helen is in my office making the sign for tea.
I nod and shoo her out.

'It's very close to the end,' I say,
speaking to her like an ordinary client.
'Last thing
is to produce estate accounts for the beneficiaries,
          namely you.
I'll set out what tax has been paid, all accounts settled,
          that sort of thing.'

'It's so complicated.
Connor was right to choose a solicitor as executor.
I was annoyed about that for a while,
like he didn't trust me.
Silly, I know.

Now I see it was sensible.
Mark would have taken twelve years to do it.'
She laughs. It is crinkled and false.

'I'll email the accounts when they're done.'

Rebecca thanks me then says,
'I'm having a few people over for dinner this weekend.
Would you like to come? Would that be strange?
Your partner is welcome.'

☙

We never argued, except about The Situation.
Anything else we tried to debate
turned into resolution,
a pact to listen,
disagree.
            You'd hold me and let me have my opinions.
It was new, exciting,
like everything else you brought with you.

But then I said,
'You should make me the executor to your will,'
and I saw something sneer in you at my presumption.

'Why would I do that?'

'Because it's my job.
And your darling wife wouldn't have to worry.'

'Don't call her that.'

'Sorry. Your bitch wife wouldn't have to worry.'
You examined a crossword puzzle in the newspaper on your lap.
You didn't have a pen.
We were in a Hampstead tea room.
The steam machine hissed and whistled.
Cups clanked.
The walls were deep red.

'I think you should change your will.
Especially when you split up.
Why should she get it all?
Put it into trust for the kids.'

'What are you talking about?
I'm not going to die, Ana.'

'Everyone's going to die, Connor.'

'What's this about?'
You folded the newspaper,
then your arms.

Whenever we made love, your hands in my hair,
your mouth on my collarbones, your breath in my ears,
I wanted to smash the world apart to keep you.
        I would have given it all up.

But that day your eyes were cold,
and I hated you for what you were making me feel.

'It's me or her,' I said.

'Fine, be the executor,
but I'm quite sure you're going first.'

'Choose.'

'What?'

'Me or Rebecca.'

'Don't do this.'

'If you choose me now but stay with her,
I'll call her and tell her everything.'

'Stop threatening me.'

'Choose.'

'Now? You want me to choose now?
This is silly. What if I don't pick you?
Then what?'

'We have a decision.'

'Ana.'

'How much longer do you need to
work out this puzzle, Connor?
You've had years.
Years to decide, years to explain it to Rebecca,
years to split up with me, if that's what you wanted.'

'Why can't you ever see it from my perspective?
It's worse for me, I—'

'Stop there. I can't listen to any more.
It's insulting. And humiliating.'

'Ana.'

'Good luck, Connor.' I stood.
I didn't touch you or say goodbye.

It was the last time I saw you.

A ticking takes me upstairs to Ruth's room.
The door is ajar.

Inside, my eldest is sitting up straight
at her desk,
the new monogrammed coloured pencils
                    she got from Santa lined up along it.

She takes each one,
snaps it in half.
Then again. Into quarters.
Sets the lot aside.

Red, snap. Red, snap, snap.

Turquoise, snap. Turquoise, snap, snap.

She is expressionless. Concentrating.

I step away so she won't see me watching
and gaze at the floor.
But I cannot ignore the sound of it –
the snapping of my child.

❧

My body gave away nothing.

No swelling or sickness.
No desire for Doritos
like the last two times.

Only an absence of aches and bleeding.

I spent an evening online
hunting out reasons for the delay.
Age. Possibly.
Stress. Yes.
Tiredness. Always.

I got a kit, just in case,
and there it was, a pass.
Positive.
Your fruit floating blue in plastic
but looking curiously
like an error –
X marks the mistake.

And so
I had
no choice,
no opportunity to practise even a
moderate morality.

I saw my GP,
then the chemist,
and took two pills
to wash away the life
we'd made,
          the you in me.
     So easy.

Sometimes I think about its little spirit,
as delicate and almost imagined
as ripples in air made by the wings of a dragonfly,
and I feel so sad
for so long.

That night Paul said, 'You're always somewhere else.'

'It's true. I'm sorry,' I said.

I went to bed with a hot-water bottle,
not bothering to kiss the kids goodnight.

☙

Rebecca opens the door.
She has pretty eyes. I never noticed them before.
'Come in!' She glances at a wall clock. 'You're the first.'

'Did you say six?'

'I did. Everyone else is late!
Late as usual. Open that, would you?' Rebecca says,
taking a bottle of white from the cooler
and attending to something on the hob.
          She forgets to give me a corkscrew.

Your boys are in the sitting room playing a video game.
Jamie turns, sees me, waves enthusiastically.
'Want a turn?' he calls out,
holding the controller aloft.

I shake my head.

The doorbell rings and David hurtles into the hall to answer it.
'Hey, trouble!' someone says.
He skids back into the kitchen followed by a couple.
The woman is tall. Red lipstick. Sequinned skirt.
The man has a scraggy beard. He is wearing a fedora.
What the fuck? Mark mouths the words at me.

Rebecca opens her arms to them.
'Hey, you made it without getting puked on!
How is the peanut?'

The woman, his wife Donna, rolls her eyes.
'Not sleeping, that's for sure.
Teething, I think. Getting on my nerves.

Why doesn't anyone warn you about babies?
But he's with his granny for the night.
And he's gorgeous.'

Mark takes a glass from Rebecca, downing half of it.

'This is Ana,' Rebecca explains.

Mark nods. 'Yeah, I know.
We met at the funeral, didn't we?
I'm Mark Dahl. I was a very good friend of Connor's.'

Rebecca frowns.
'You were at the funeral? You never said.'

The room watches. Waits for an answer.
And somewhere you are seeing this too.

'I was there to represent the firm,' I say.
'I hope that was OK.'
I taste the wine. 'This is lovely.'

Donna clacks across the kitchen to a bowl of olives.
'Who else is coming?' she asks.
'Not your bloody cousin, I hope.
She's so clever and cultured.
I'm going to start reading again, I really am.
At the very least, I'm going to buy some books.'

Mark pulls a packet of cigarettes from his blazer pocket.
'Join me,' he says,
nodding at the garden.
What choice have I but to follow him?

Outside
he is standing next to the nicer-than-normal shed –
cedar wood, sedum roof.
He lights a cigarette, inhales and hands it to me.
'I don't know what's going on here but after tonight
you're to fuck off. Do you understand?'

The grass has a frosty film but I don't feel cold
despite the sheer shirt I am wearing.
I suck on the cigarette, stagger.
'It's curious how you've suddenly acquired moral leanings
on the subject of infidelity.
You never cared before.
You condoned it.
Colluded.'

'Do you fucking understand?'

I exhale into the night. It is black. Starry.
And I am nothing beneath it.
'Of course, I understand.'

'You've no right to be here.
I genuinely don't get it.'

'Me neither.'
I have looked and I have not found you here.
I have looked and you are nowhere.
You are gone.

'The Wilsons have turned up. Don't leave me with them.'
It's Donna behind us, halfway up the garden.

Mark turns to me.
'Tell Rebecca you got an emergency call from home.
You aren't welcome.'

'What?' Donna shouts.

I hand Mark my wine glass and head inside.

Rebecca is laughing with a young couple –
        both of them fashionable and loud,
            the woman in the middle of an anecdote.
Rebecca seems slight next to the couple.

'And I told him, it's an Andy Warhol, you twat,'
the woman concludes.
'I mean, an Andy Warhol!'
Everyone laughs and I momentarily consider
divulging my own story – finding something to amuse them.
'Who's this?' The man turns to me.

'This is Ana,' Rebecca says. 'She's been given the night off.'
I touch her arm. The cotton is so soft
I want to keep my fingers there.
'I have to shoot, I'm afraid.
The kids are puking.'

'No, that's such a shame.'
Rebecca glances at the table worriedly,
as though thinking about a seating plan.
        I helped with even numbers.
But she spots my handbag on a chair,
sees my phone poking out of the pocket.
'How do you know they're sick?'

'Look, Rebecca, I shouldn't have come.'

Mark and Donna blunder back into the kitchen.
Mark stamps his feet on the mat.
'Freezing my balls off out there,' he says.
He looks at me. 'Still here?'

Rebecca wags a finger. 'Did he offend you?
He's a knob most of the time, you should ignore him.'

'Knob!' Jamie shouts out, cackling,
his face smeared with pizza sauce.

'It's true though. He's utterly obnoxious.
Aren't you, Mark? It's part of your boyish charm.'
Rebecca finds the wine bottle and refills his glass.

'And what's Ana's redeeming feature?' he asks.

'I should go,' I say.

'Yeah,' Mark mutters. 'Before the party really gets started.'

The song on the speaker ends
and there is no music in the room
and no speaking
and everyone is examining me
apart from Rebecca, who is confused and reaching for
my hands.
She takes them in her own.
'Please come another time.
Being a mother is endless.'
There is genuine concern in her tone now
and I realise the dinner is of no consequence –
this panic is grief
and it is real,
and lasting,
and it is because she loves you
and you have left
and nothing makes sense any more.

'Goodnight,' I say. 'Thank you.
I'm sorry. I really am.'

Rebecca walks me to the door.
'Whatever it is, I hope you're OK,' she says,
and kisses me lightly.

Over her shoulder, Mark is eyeballing me.
And Donna is stroking his neck.

∾

It hurt so much I couldn't go home,
our baby bleeding out of me on to my clothes
and the desk chair.
Tanya said, 'You look terrible.'

I was sweating, couldn't remember much.
When everyone had gone home
I sat with my back to the wall and hugged my knees.
I woke in the early morning to silence, my skirt soaking.

And I called you.
'I need you,' I said. 'I really need you.'

You whispered so you wouldn't be overheard.
'Where are you? What's happened?'

I explained and you listened.
And I knew you were crying for this thing
you hadn't realised existed and was now gone
and for my pain
and for what we had done to one another.
'Oh, God, Ana. Oh God.'

But when I said again, 'I need you,'
you were quiet.

And you did not come to me.

∽

In the raw dark garden
the moonbeams light me up
like I am on a stage.
But I am not singing or dancing.

I press my palms against the gnarled
bark of the fruitless plum tree
in my garden and stare into the sky.

There is nothing else.

∽

I showered off the dried blood
that had crusted along my legs.
           Paul was at work.
I was waiting for Nora,
had told her I'd miscarried.

You called and I said,
'You're a prick,' by way of greeting.
       I meant it.
You were cruel. A liar.
You were never leaving.
And I meant everything else too.
       'You don't know what love looks like.
       I can't trust you.
       I can't carry on like this.'

I meant everything
            in that last conversation.

What I don't know
is whether you meant your last words too.
       'I love you, Ana.
       I'm so sorry you've had to do this alone.
       It'll never happen again. I promise.
       I'm doing my best.
           I am.
           It isn't enough, but I'm trying.
           And I'll try harder.'

I put down the phone, couldn't listen any more
to the hollow clamour of our arguments.

You tried to call back.
You tried three more times.

I didn't answer.
If I had done, you would still be alive.

Prick.

∾

Fifteen minutes after I'd slammed down the phone,
a van knocked you off your bike
on Alexandra Park Road
as you cycled towards my home.

If I had given you another thirty seconds.
If I had let you speak.
If I had answered a call.

It is not my fault, I have told myself.

But.
I could not listen.
I could no longer believe.

∾

'And one last question,' I said. 'How did he die?'

Rebecca told me, briefly, all about the bike accident.

I put down the phone and bought a pair of shoes online.

Then I opened up your will
and changed it,
made myself the executor,
        which you never got around to doing,
so I could know your life
and befriend your wife
and keep you for a while.

Then I got back to work.
I have never worn the stupid shoes.

ᐁ

Your brass plaque is clean.
I press my forehead to its coldness.
I am sorry I have not visited before.
I am sorry I have left you alone here.

You will never leave, but I will.
I will catch the bus home, make dinner for my children.
I will try to finish *Anna Karenina*, and occasionally get manicures.

I am sorry that by the end I could not hear you or give you time
or accept the love I knew was real and mine
and secret and sickening and something
I never felt worthy of receiving.

Before you, I lurched through life
thinking I could be happy if I was good.
You made me very bad, Connor.
And I am so glad.

I have been looking for you everywhere else.
You have been here all the time, waiting.
       Is she with you? Our little fluttering?
You knew I would come.
And I have.
But I will have to leave.
I will have to be brave and bad again.

I'm sorry I never said you were beautiful.
       I was too ashamed to describe you that way.
But you were.
          So beautiful.

I am sorry for it all, Connor.

ॐ

At the gates to the cemetery, Rebecca is climbing out of a taxi.
She spots me and waves.

'Ana! Gosh, this is a surprise.'
She hugs me, smelling of shampoo.
'I come every week.
I didn't know you had someone here too,' she says.
'Are you alright?
You left so suddenly the other night.'

I want to tell her,
to drop to my knees, envelop her
and ask forgiveness, share the weight.
            You are so heavy.
But there is no need for dramatic declarations
because Rebecca is staring at my hands,
at her blue leather gloves,
and knows everything,
or at least she will later on
when this scene settles within her.
'Rebecca … ' I try.

'I should go in,' she says, unable to smile.

Roses jut from the top of her tote bag.
                  A gift.
Maybe you would have preferred some shamrock.
But I hope she will lay them down for you anyway.

'Goodbye,' she says.

❧

The children are asleep.
Paul is marking a stack of books.
We have not spoken in several days.
I lean on him.

'I love someone else,' I say.

He puts down his pen. 'Who?'

'He's gone now.'

'Where has he gone?'

'Just gone.'
I am crying, hoping Paul will not shout and wake the children.

He takes my thumb between his fingers.
'Sit down,' he says. 'And talk to me.'

About the Author

Sarah Crossan has lived in Dublin, London, and New York, and she now lives in Hertfordshire. She graduated with a degree in philosophy and literature before training as an English and drama teacher at Cambridge University. *The Weight of Water* and *Apple and Rain* were both shortlisted for the CILIP Carnegie Medal. In 2016, Crossen won the CILIP Carnegie Medal as well as the YA Book Prize, the CBI Book of the Year award and the CLiPPA Poetry Award for her novel *One*.